THE HARVESTING SERIES

THE
SHADOW
ASPECT

MELANIE
KARSAK

Published by Clockpunk Press
PO Box 560367
Rockledge, FL 32956-0367

CLOCKPUNK PRESS
Cover art by Princess of Shadows
Editing by Becky Stephens Editing
Book design by Inkstain Interior Book Designing
Text set in Cochin LT.

for Michael

THE SHADOW ASPECT

LAYLA

I don't like roller coasters. One summer, Ian convinced me to join Jaime and some girlfriend of his at the time on a road trip to "the best coaster park in the world." It was one of those days that lives on in memory as a collage of color, laughter, and sketchy detail. What I do remember is that Ian wasted nearly twenty dollars trying to win me an over-sized teddy bear. He never won it. I also remember Jaime and his girlfriend making out in the backseat the entire ride home. We could hear the wet sounds of their kisses over the Nazareth tunes Ian had cranking on the radio.

The old wooden coasters weren't as bad. They rattled you hard, but you never felt like you were out of control. Ian, however, coerced me into riding a sleek, modern coaster that pulled 3Gs. Of course, he didn't tell me that before I got on the ride. I remember opening my eyes and seeing my feet and the sky all at once. The next moment, I was staring face down at the ground while my stomach lunged toward my throat. When we got off, my hands and legs shook. Ian teased me. Jaime wandered off only to return with a five-dollar bottle of Sprite for me. I'd hated feeling like I'd momentarily allowed someone else to dictate if I lived or died.

When I took the final step into the labyrinth, I felt that same massive tug, a throttling feeling like I was out of control, and an enormous heave forward. A kaleidoscope of color thundered past my eyes and a booming sound rattled in my ears. But somewhere in the middle of all that color and light, things stopped for a brief moment, and I found myself standing in a misty forest. The trees there, pink dogwoods, were in full bloom. As I inhaled, the blossoms got larger. As I exhaled, the blossoms got smaller. It was if the whole world was expanding and contracting on the command of my breath.

"Layla?" a woman's voice called.

I paused and looked around. Thick, white vapor had enveloped nearly everything.

"Layla?" she called again. This time, I saw a tall figure moving toward me. I recognized Peryn.

"Peryn? Here! I'm here."

The mists around us began to clear. I saw Peryn clearly. The look on her face startled me. She looked horrified. "Oh, Layla," she called, trying to reach for me, wading through the mists as if they were pushing heavily against her, "you must not trust—" she began, but her words were drowned out by screams.

I turned toward the shouting to see figures moving toward me. It was strange. It was like I was seeing people walking around inside smoke. I was near them, but they remained hidden in shadow. Thin places. I was in one of the thin places that Grandma Petrovich had always spoken of. I could see my world, but I was not present in it. My world was like a shadow layer over the other world, the world of the spirit, where I now resided. I squinted hard. I thought I could see trees…and I could see Jaime's silhouette. There were others around him—Summer, Ethel, Will. Their voices sounded muffled. Dark shadows ambled toward them.

"Layla," Peryn called, her voice barely audible.

I turned to see fog engulf Peryn. She was gone. In her place, the mists began to clear. I could smell the forest. The scents of pine and the decay of earth assailed my nose. I felt that same pull again, and I was thrust forward, pitching out of the thin place with a heave. Dumped unceremoniously back into my world, I found myself lying facedown on the leaf-covered ground. The deep, loamy smell of soil filled my nose. It was dark. My head was spinning, but one thing was certain, I could hear screams.

Kiki's face appeared above me as she tried to pull me off the ground. Everything was distorted and fuzzy. She was shouting at me, but I couldn't make out her words. My mind was a rattled confusion of sound. Kiki's eyes darted around wildly. She was yelling and pulling my arms, lifting me off the ground. In the dim moonlight, I saw the flash of gunfire. It was then that I realized that I heard a lot of gunfire. I looked around, trying to make out what I was seeing, but everything was in a haze. Larry, who was standing over us, fired his shotgun. In the light of the discharge, I saw one of the undead coming up on him.

"Layla, get up! Now!" Kiki's voice finally broke through.

The undead man lunged at me. Larry cracked him on the side of the head with the butt of his rifle but two more appeared out of nowhere. In the dim light, I watched in horror as they pulled Larry to the ground. His feet thrashed wildly as they ripped him apart. He screamed a blood-curdling howl. Gunfire blasted all around me.

"Larry!" I heard Ethel wail.

"Larry?" I croaked.

A gunshot blasted. Larry's feet went still.

Kiki pulled me up and began dragging me away. As we moved through the darkness, I could see several of the undead feasting on what was left of Dusty. His eyes were frozen open wide as the undead tore into his stomach.

"Kiki, Layla, come on," Will screamed. The others had collected away from the scene and were retreating into the woods. The woods? Where were we?

"Layla," I heard Jaime call weakly.

The undead were everywhere. And we were nowhere. I took in the scene. We were in the middle of the forest but not on the island and not in Hamletville. Tall trees silhouetted the nights' sky. Dim moonlight provided the only light to be had. We had emerged in the depths of a thick glen. The undead were all over the place. Everywhere I looked people I knew were being pulled to the ground, being ripped limb from limb, consumed by the hungry mouths of the undead.

Mrs. Finch went under with an inhuman wail as they took massive bites out of her neck and head. Buddie, Will, and a barely-alert Jaime circled around Frenchie, the girls, Ethel, and Summer. They shot at the undead as they backed away from the horde, moving into the dark woods. Moments later, I couldn't even see them anymore. But I could see the undead, and they were everywhere. The sharp scent of their rotting flesh, a smell like body odor and rotted meat, assailed my nose. My head pounded. I felt like someone was blaring heavy metal music while I was in the middle of open heart surgery.

I pulled myself together. I had to or Kiki and I, separated from the rest of the group, were going to die. For a moment, the terror of it felt very real. My heart slammed in my chest.

"I'm okay," I lied. "I'm okay. Let's go," I told her. In a state of shock, I gripped my shashka, and we started to fight through the crowd. What the hell had happened? The fox woman said the gateway would take us off the island. Clearly, it had, but why hadn't it taken us somewhere safe? It was at that moment, as the undead moved toward Kiki and me, that I realized a terrible truth. We had been lied to, manipulated. The fox woman had tricked us. I had led my people into an ambush. What had I expected, that we would pass through the labyrinth and find ourselves back in Hamletville or in some sort of paradise? Did I really think we'd find ourselves somewhere safe? Why? Just because she wasn't human, because she had seemed kind? The reality was before me now. Nothing was further from the truth. We had emerged at the gates of hell, and it was no accident.

"Layla," Jaime called from the darkness.

"They're everywhere." Kiki swore as she shot at a group of undead.

Almost on instinct, my shashka swung, stabbing a slobbering undead man in tattered rags who grabbed at me. Kiki and I moved deeper into the forest following the others. In the dim light, I saw the undead fighting over the remains of the hotel survivors and Hamletville citizens. My heart broke. This wasn't supposed to happen. We were supposed to end up somewhere safe.

Getting some distance between us and the undead feasting on corpses, Kiki and I cut and ran. We sprinted and soon joined the others, dodging the undead milling about between us and the rest of the group. There were less than a dozen of us. Was that it? Were we the only ones who survived?

"We need to get out of here," Kiki said as she reloaded her gun.

"We're in the middle of nowhere," Summer exclaimed, her face pale from fright. Blood was streaked across her cheek.

"This way," Buddie said with certainty as he quickly scanned the horizon.

The group bolted behind him. Tom grabbed Kira, and Will took Susan from Frenchie's arms. Everyone sprinted into the darkness behind Buddie. The undead had already started to advance on us once more.

For just a moment, I looked back. We really *were* in the middle of nowhere. The woods was very thick, the trees old and massive. In the distance, I noticed a cave in the side of a mountain. This is where we had emerged. It was the gateway. The stones around the cave gave off an unnatural blue glow, just as the labyrinth stones had done. In the pale blue light surrounding the cave entrance, for just a moment, I saw the shadowed silhouette of a fox.

I took a step toward her.

"Layla, come on," Jaime called.

We hustled through the woods, but the undead were everywhere. One jumped at Ethel. She screamed. In a flash, Summer stabbed the undead woman through the eye with my hunting knife. The walking corpse toppled to the ground.

"Layla, your guns?" Will called.

I pulled the guns out. Water dripped from them. I shook them out and prayed they would fire. I passed off my handguns to the others. The automatic barely had twenty rounds left.

We huddled together and made our way through the darkness. Gunshots blasted as we spent the last of the ammo. We pushed forward, but soon we could see the shadows of another horde coming toward us. Behind us, we could hear the lumbering sounds as the massive group of undead pursued us. Everywhere I looked, hordes of the undead narrowed in on us. Stunned, we all simply stood. No one knew what to do.

Susan whimpered.

"Mommy," Kira cried, her scared little voice piercing our terrified silence.

My heart broke. This was my fault. This was all my fault. I had trusted too blindly.

I turned to look at Frenchie. In the dim twilight, I saw tears streaming from her eyes.

I reached out for Jaime.

Then, through the darkness, I heard a strange sound. At first I was not sure what it was. A moment later, however, I made out the soft purr of an engine coming from somewhere ahead of us.

"What is that?" Kiki asked.

I listened. The sound of the engine grew louder. Then, I saw headlights. "There," I yelled, pointing. Dodging the oncoming horde, we raced toward the approaching vehicle. Afraid we would miss it, Will, the fastest of us, handed Susan to Tom and took off toward the vehicle.

A dozen or so of the undead reached the back of the group. The others shot; out of ammo, I swung. The undead pushed against us as we retreated toward the headlights. Kira screamed as one of the undead caught her by the arm.

Fred Johnson hit the undead man with a baseball bat. It let go of Kira, but lunged at Fred, biting him on the head. He went down with a scream.

"Fred," I called and reached out for him.

The tips of his fingers just brushed against mine, but the undead were faster. They swarmed in on him. He was lost.

Jaime, blood dripping down his forehead, came from behind and pulled me away. "Come on!"

We ran forward. Soon we could make out the edge of a road. The headlights rolled toward us. Will ran out onto the road and waved his arms. In the glow of the headlights, the shape of the truck grew clearer.

"That's a military transport," Jaime said.

We ran toward the road. Moments later, we heard the rattle of machine gun fire. Someone in the truck was shooting. The undead closing in on us fell to the ground.

Frantic, breathless, and in shock, what was left of my group emerged at the side of the road.

The driver slowed the truck. "Y'all better shake a leg if you wanna live," a young, blonde-haired woman called from the driver's seat. In the back, a young man with long dreadlocks shot at the horde.

Quickly, we all loaded into the back of the truck. Kira and Susan settled in beside Frenchie. Ethel, out of breath and clinging to Summer, nearly collapsed onto the flatbed.

The machine gun rattled. When the last of us were loaded in, the driver gunned the engine. We sped into the darkness. Ahead, the path was clear. Everyone sat looking at the road behind us. In the moonlight, we could see the horde of undead lumber onto the road, but their shadows receded as we drove away.

I closed my eyes and took a deep breath. I looked up at Jaime. We were alive. We had been through hell, someone had seen to that, but we were alive. We had been deceived. No, I had been deceived, but we were alive. Jaime put his hands on my cheeks and kissed me hard. We were alive.

When he let go, I turned and looked at the others. Everyone was in a state of shock. Ethel was weeping on Summer's shoulder. Kiki sat in the back of the truck, her knees pulled tight to her chest, her head buried in her arms. Will, Buddie, and Tom stared blankly into the darkness.

I took a deep breath, rose, and made my way to the front of the truck. The window in the back had been broken out.

"Thank you so much," I told the driver. "We would have died out there."

"Gotta save the living," the girl said then stuck her hand over her shoulder toward me. "I'm Cricket. That's Chase."

Chase nodded to me, his sharp eyes never venturing far from the woods around us.

"Layla," I replied.

"So, just what are you doin' in the middle of the woods, Layla?" she asked.

"With kids," Chase added.

"It's a long story," I replied, unsure what to say. "How did you find us?"

"It's a long story," Cricket replied with a laugh.

Chase chuckled.

"Doesn't matter either way. Get settled in. Assumin' no more zombies try to eat us tonight, we'll be home soon," Cricket said.

"This is a military transport, isn't it? Is there military where you are?"

Cricket laughed loudly. "No. There is no military anymore. Hang in there. You'll be safe soon."

I sat back down beside Jaime and rested my head on his shoulder. I then said a silent prayer to whomever would listen. I had been wrong. People were dead. People I was obligated to protect had been eaten alive because I had trusted...a shapeshifter? A fox woman? Regardless, I had trusted the wrong person. I felt like I was walking blind. Whatever I thought I had learned to see was not enough. I couldn't see anything, and now so many of us were gone.

Guilt washed over me. I'd been so blind. My arrogance had gotten in the way. Just because I hadn't been fooled by Rumor's people didn't mean I was special. All it meant was that vampire glamour had no effect on me. When it came down to it, I was a fool. I'd believed that the enemy of my enemy was my friend. All my life, I'd never learned who to trust. I always put my faith in people's words, assuming they meant what they said, just like I did. Wasn't everyone else just like me, good on the inside? Over and over again, I had believed lies: my mother's, Ian's, and so many in between. I had danced with the devil all the while wondering why I was still in hell. And this time, I had paid for my misguided trust with blood.

My grandmother, who could always see the other world, told me I had to truly see. I saw through the vampires, but didn't see through the bigger trap. The truth was, mankind was now at the bottom of the food chain. Vampires were not the only ones after us. If I was going to keep those I loved safe, I could never trust again.

LAYLA

The military transport clattered through the darkness down a bumpy dirt road for about an hour before making a turn onto a paved rural route. The headlights shone into the empty expanse. Overhead, the stars glimmered, unaware of our despair. Cricket sang "These Boots Are Made for Walkin'" with more gusto than seemed fitting, or, perhaps, to spite the despair that prevailed. Occasionally we would come upon one of the undead lumbering along the road. Cricket would slow, and Chase would fire.

Just as the first rays of sunlight began to break through the clouds, Cricket drove the transport up a ramp and onto the interstate. The moment I saw the sun, relief washed over me. At least the creatures of the night could not menace us — for now. The interstate ramp had been cleared, but abandoned cars packed the road. Maneuvering carefully between vehicles, Cricket pulled the truck onto the grassy median and drove west. The interstate proved a ghastly sight.

Everyone stared wide-eyed at the remains of the world around us. Burned out cars, dead bodies, and other "stuff" that had once seemed so important were strewn everywhere. I cast a glance at Kira and Susan, both of whom slept under the protection of their mother's arms. I was glad they couldn't see this. Sheltered in Hamletville, we hadn't seen the world burn. What was left of humanity looked a lot like a garbage heap. The smell of death, wafting scents of gasoline, rotted food, and decaying bodies was pungent.

I looked up at Jaime. His eyes were closed. I knew it wasn't the death of the world that plagued him but the loss of Ian. His brother was gone.

I leaned against him. After all Ian had done wrong, in the end he had sacrificed himself for me, for Jaime, for all of us. Whatever Rumor and the others had turned Ian into, it was not strong enough to break the bonds of love he had felt.

My thoughts were broken by a peppering of gunfire. Neither Kira nor Susan woke. A small group of the undead had been meandering on the highway. Chase made short work of them. But it was not, it seemed, the undead that most interested him. Chase was looking intently at the row of cars in the east-bound lane.

"Slow up," he called to Cricket.

"See somethin'?" she called.

The transport slowed to a stop. The majority of my group looked drowsy eyed, but Buddie and Will perked up. I stood and joined Chase. Cricket put the truck into park and slid through the back window.

"You suppose…" Chase asked Cricket, his question indicating we'd missed the conversation. They both stared at a large semi-truck parked in the east-bound lane. An image painted on the trailer depicted two crossed swords.

Cricket frowned, looking annoyed. "Well, I reckon we can look."

"What is it?" Buddie asked.

"We'll check the cargo in that semi," Chase answered as he unholstered his handguns.

Cricket checked her revolver then reached into the cab of the truck to pull out the largest wrench I'd ever seen.

"We can help," I told them. I wanted to see what had them so interested.

Chase and Cricket exchanged a debating glance.

"All right, but someone who can drive this thing needs to stay back," Cricket said.

"I'll stay," Jaime said absently. He never looked up.

With that, Will, Buddie, Cricket, Chase and I jumped out of the truck and crossed the grass toward the semi.

"Are you expecting to find something in particular?" I asked.

"Playing a hunch," Chase replied.

I looked at Cricket. The girl's curly strawberry-blonde hair shined in the morning light. Where ever they were staying, they were able to keep themselves clean and they both looked nourished. But, no matter how she looked physically, her expression told me even more about her. She wasn't into playing hunches.

As we crossed the grass, two of the undead emerged. Buddie shot an arrow at the one closest to the truck while Will stabbed the other through the eye. Chase and Cricket watched us with curiosity. I got the feeling they were assessing us too. When we got to the truck, Cricket worked on the lock with her wrench.

"Need help?" I asked.

"Nah. She'll come. Rusted out," she said with a grunt. A moment later, the lock popped. The chain hit the ground, and Cricket unlatched the door, pushing the trailer open. The truck was mostly empty. In the very back, however, there was a small pile of boxes.

Cricket crawled into the truck. Will and I followed.

The boxes had no markings. Cricket kneeled to open them.

"Need a knife?" Will offered, handing Cricket his Swiss army knife.

She smiled at him, took the knife, and then opened the boxes.

Out of the corner of my eye, I saw Will looking her over. I could tell he liked what he saw. A moment later, Cricket gasped.

"Well, I'll be," she said under her breath as she pulled out an insulated package that was marked hazardous. From inside, she removed a white box and looked it over. I couldn't quite see what it was, but it look like vials of medicine.

"Crick?" Chase called into the trailer.

"Yep?" Cricket answered, sticking the package into a bag she had strung around her body.

"Well?

"It's here."

"Unbelievable," Chase muttered.

"You know Vella," Cricket called.

"Someone sent you here?" I asked.

"You could say that," Cricket replied, a perplexed look on her face, but she didn't say more, and I didn't ask.

Inside the other boxes, we found bandages, splints, and other medical supplies.

"Give me a hand with these?" Cricket asked Will.

"Of course," he replied.

Will and Cricket grabbed all the boxes and headed out of the trailer. I followed behind. Chase took most of the boxes from Cricket and, chatting in low tones, the two of them headed back toward the transport, Will dragging along behind.

Buddie waited for me. "What do you think?" he asked as we set off across the grass.

"They aren't vampires."

He smiled wryly. "They look all right."

"Agreed, but something's up. There were meds in those boxes, and it seems like they knew they were there."

"Maybe someone sent them after the truck, knew about it. Meds might be hard to come by where they are. After all, they didn't have Grandma Petrovich to stockpile for them."

I grinned at his joke but still felt uncomfortable. "Yeah, well, we'll see," I replied.

Cricket and Chase quickly loaded the boxes into the cab, and Cricket set off again. We drove a while before Cricket turned the truck off the highway and across a field. The ground was damp; the fresh green grasses and spring flowers filled the air with a tangy, earthy smell. Cricket followed a stream south. After some drive, we came across a small, rural bridge. She pulled the truck across the bridge and followed a back road into the woods. The sunlight shone through the trees as mist rose upward. The rays of sun, scattered in the mist, glimmered gold. Soon, the grade of the road dropped, and we started winding down the side of a mountain. As the road snaked around the hillside, the mists began to clear. We entered a small valley, a large lake at its center. Around us, the trees were loaded with spring buds. I started seeing rooftops and church steeples.

It was already after midday. Everyone was awake and alert now, watching, waiting. We soon found ourselves driving into a small town much like Hamletville. A road post, really an old granite boulder, had "Welcome to Ulster, Maryland" chiseled on it. Above the wording, a small four-leafed clover had been carved into the rock. How in the hell did we end up in Maryland?

We drove through the abandoned town. Before everything had died, the town must have been rather quaint. Small boutiques, cafés, pubs, bookstores, bed and breakfasts, and other small shops lined the streets. The sidewalks had been laid with cobblestone, and the streetlights were antique-looking gaslight replicas. A faded and tattered banner advertising an Autumn Leaf Festival was strung over the main thoroughfare. The streets were completely empty. The town looked like it had been cleaned up. Cars had been moved to the side. Business doors were locked with chains and padlocks. Through the windows, you could see that shelves were bare. The place was a ghost town, a shadow of its former self.

The truck rolled through town. No undead stirred. At the far end of town, Cricket turned onto a side street and drove up a very steep hill. At its top, she made a hard right. Poised above the town, we found ourselves outside the gates of a locked and guarded...castle?

We all strained to get a better look. On further inspection, I noticed a bronze plaque on the stone gatepost: Claddagh-Basel College.

"A college?" Tom wondered aloud.

Chase laughed. "Castle, more like. Brought over brick by brick from Ireland, or so we we've been told about a hundred times," Chase said, shooting Cricket a glance.

The girl giggled.

"Hell of a place, though," Chase continued. "It's walled all the way around. We've got guards on the gate and patrolling the fence. So far, we've been able to keep it safe."

I looked at the fence. It was made of stone up to about eight feet in height. Above that was another five feet of wrought-iron fence. Fleur-de-lis designs at the top made effective spikes. The building was a massive fortress.

The two men who had been standing guard unbolted the gate and let us in.

Cricket drove up the driveway and parked the truck in front of the main building at the center of the complex. A stone staircase led toward arched double doors. The keystone above the door bore the Claddagh symbol, a crowned heart held by two hands. Cricket parked the truck behind two other military vehicles.

"Was the military here?" Jaime asked.

Chase shook his head. "No, we found the trucks abandoned. Just the trucks, guns, and a whole lot of ramen noodles left behind."

"Remember when Kellimore's skin turned yellow from the dye in the flavor packets? I guess when you eat noodles every day, the food colorin' catches up with you," Cricket said with a laugh that Chase joined. "Come on, y'all look like you could use some noodles and a stiff drink. Layla, right?"

I nodded.

"Welcome to Claddagh-Basel."

LAYLA

Who survives the apocalypse? Would the most dangerous on Darwin's food chain dominate the rest of us? Would it be the cleverest or the best armed? In Hamletville, we were a family. We protected the fragile. But, outside of Hamletville, what would we find?

Cricket and Chase led us through a side entrance on the first floor. The place was eerily silent. The walls were bare and painted white, the floor tiles olive-colored. It was dim in the hallway. Cricket pulled out a flashlight and led the way.

"Boiler rooms, labs, offices. When we got here, we had to help clear out a few zombies. Grizzly mess," she said then flashed the light on the blood-stained walls.

"No one stays in this corridor," Chase added. "At least, not to sleep. Too cold."

"Speaking of which," Cricket said then dug in her bag. She pulled out the package she'd found in the truck and handed it to Chase. "Will you do the honors?"

Chase grinned. "You sure you don't want to deliver it?"

Cricket shook her head. "Let her know I'm takin' them out to the library?"

He nodded to Cricket then turned to us. "I'll see you all later," he said then headed down a side corridor to one of the labs. I noticed a light shining out from under the door.

"This way," Cricket said.

We made our way to a stairwell. The plaster on the walls was chipping off in large clumps. Dusty statuary of saints and the Virgin Mary were tucked in small alcoves, candles at their feet.

"You'll find candles laying around just about everywhere you turn in this place," Cricket said then. "There is a small chapel in the main building."

As we turned the corner at the second floor landing, Cricket nearly collided with a hulking man.

"Dammit," he swore, his flashlight hitting the floor with a thud.

The flashlight rolled to my feet. I picked it up and handed it to the stranger. He was a young man, no older than twenty, with a wicked scar running from his temple to the corner of his mouth.

"Christ, Cricket, you scared me half to death," he said then as he sized us up. "Who are they?"

"Chase and I went out for supplies, came across their group."

The young man flashed his light on all of us. I saw Ethel wince when the light shone in her face.

"Lower your light," I said then. The edge on my voice was hard. "We've got women and children here."

Cricket reached out and pushed the light down. "I got this. Go on with whatever you were doing."

"I'm just interested in security."

"Yeah, I know," Cricket said then rolled her eyes. "Come on, Layla. This way," she said, then led us up another two flights of steps to the fourth floor.

When the young man was out of earshot, Cricket turned to me and said, "That's Kellimore. Local kid. He was the town football hero, some kind of hotshot before the world went to hell. He can act like a jerk, but, that said, he saved most of the townies here. Doctor Gustav keeps him in line."

"Who is Doctor Gustav?" I asked.

"One of the people in charge here," Cricket answered.

We wound up the steps to the fourth floor. Cricket led us down a quiet corridor. The walls, made of thick, polished wood, gave an air of age to the place. Photographs of students in sports jerseys lined the walls, their varied hairstyles—from the ridiculous to what had a year before been considered fashionable—showed the passage of time. The students' smiling faces brought back a flood of memories of a life now obliterated. Fencing tournaments, diets, workouts at the gym, it all seemed like a joke. Now that every moment, every decision, could be your last, everything that had come before was starting to feel a lot like decadent masturbation.

As we walked, I heard a flood of footsteps running from a side corridor toward us, a tinkling of small bells echoing the steps. Moments later, a dark-haired woman appeared in the hallway. Her mountain of black hair fell to her waist. She stared at me, at the shashka at my side, then turned and looked at Cricket. They both smiled.

"All right now, sister," Cricket said, slapping her a low five as she passed.

"Welcome," the woman told us.

I picked on up her accent at once. Romanian, maybe? Still shell-shocked from the encounter with Rumor's group, I looked sharply at her. The harshness of my gaze seemed to startle her.

"Catch you later?" Cricket said to the woman who nodded.

She stood in the hallway and watched us go.

"I'll take you to the library until the doc gets a chance to come by. All the dorms and classrooms are full. Y'all can bunk in there unless she says otherwise."

"Doctor? Like a professor?" Will asked.

Cricket shook her head. "She's a regular doctor, but she was doing research here," she replied. "What's your name?"

"Will."

"*Will* you come with me after I get your folks settled in to grab some supplies?"

He smiled. "Sure."

Cricket led us to the library. The room was flooded with light. Large floor to ceiling windows looked out and over the campus green and the town below. Kira and Susan ran to the glass and pressed their faces against the window.

Cricket giggled. "Two more kids downstairs, a boy and a girl," she told Frenchie. "They'll be real glad your girls are here. Probably need to get those girls something else to wear. Want me to bring somethin'? Those dresses look thin, and it gets cold in the building at night. Don't want them gettin' sick."

Frenchie shifted awkwardly. It wasn't like she had dressed her children like that. She opened and closed her mouth about three times, trying to find the right words, but in the end she just said, "thank you."

"Not many folks come around. Should be pretty quiet. Lots of study rooms to bunk in. Just find a spot and get settled in. I'll be back in a bit. Doc should be by soon. Will?"

Will shot me a glance before he turned to follow Cricket.

I nodded in approval. Though my instincts were in doubt, Cricket seemed honest. I hoped I was right. And I did want someone to scout out the scene. Will's eyes were always sharp.

The rest of us gathered at a group of couches and sat down. At once, I felt overcome by exhaustion. Jaime sat beside me, but he still wasn't saying anything. I took his hand. It was ice cold. I realized then that he was probably in shock.

At first, we were silent. No one knew how to begin. What could we possibly say about everything that had happened in the last twenty-four hours? How could I explain myself?

I didn't know what to say, so I simply spoke the truth. "I'm sorry," I began. Some looked me in the eye, some didn't. "We are alive, but we were betrayed. I trusted the wrong person. Someone told me she would help us, that she would get us off that island. We were used. We were used to clear out those..." I paused and looked around me. Christ, even I knew I sounded crazy.

"Those vampires," Buddie said quietly.

"Oh, Jaime. Ian..." Summer said.

They had all seen what had happened, had seen how we had made it out alive. If not for Ian's sacrifice, we'd likely all be dead.

Jaime nodded, but sat studying his hands.

"Layla, how did you find that place? That labyrinth?" Frenchie asked.

"I was led there by...well...like a kind of Earth spirit."

There was silence.

"Earth spirit?" Kiki finally asked. She raised an eyebrow at me.

"It wasn't the first one I've seen. There are others in Hamletville who are good."

Again, there was silence. Their faces told me they wanted to believe.

"I've seen them too...in Hamletville...the white doe woman," Buddie said then.

Surprised, everyone looked at him.

He shrugged. "We've all seen odd things, haven't we? Weird shadows where there shouldn't be shadows. Things moving or making noise when they shouldn't. We're quick to dismiss those other things because we don't want to believe. But they are out there. I saw her a few times deep in the woods behind the Petrovich property."

"Did she ever speak to you?" I asked Buddie.

"No, but she smiled at me once," he said, then grinned abashed.

"Peryn," I said. "Her name is Peryn." And I had seen Peryn in the thin place between the labyrinth and the forest. She tried to warn me, but of what?

"Why would Earth spirits want to help us? After all, we've nearly trashed this planet," Kiki remarked bitterly.

She asked a good question. Tom started to comment when the library door opened, cutting him off before he could speak. A middle-aged woman in a white lab coat entered. She was thin, her dark-blonde hair pulled back into a tidy bun. She smiled nicely, but her eyes were hard and gray. Something about the disparity between these two images bothered me.

"I'm Doctor Gustav," the blonde woman said then. She looked us over. "Is this all of you?"

"One of our people went to help Cricket," I told the woman as I rose. I stood between my group and this newcomer. Never again.

The doctor did not miss the gesture. She smiled, her lips pulling into thin strings across her face when she did. "I see. You have weapons," she stated more than asked, looking us over.

"We do," Tom told her.

I turned to look at Tom. He too was standing.

The doctor considered us.

Kira and Susan hurried away from the window to huddle around their mother.

The doctor looked back. "Anyone injured?"

No one said a word.

"Nothing serious," I finally replied.

"And your name?"

"What's with all the questions?"

The doctor's eyes softened. "As you can guess, not everyone who finds us is a good fit for this place. We are good people. What you see is what you get. We aren't looking for problems, and I don't abide problems."

"We're not looking for trouble. We're just..." I began then paused, unsure what to say.

"We're just lost," Ethel finished.

The doctor smiled at her. "Well, now you're found. We've been here since the pandemic began, and we have managed to keep this place safe. Never hurts to have a bit more muscle around, even though the zombies seem to be slowing down a bit. I'll find a good use for all of you. The library is yours," she said then turned and stalked out of the library.

"So much for bedside manner," Tom remarked.

Just then, Cricket and Will returned with water, a heap of blankets, clothes, and a case of animal crackers.

"We've got a supply room downstairs," Cricket said as she heaved her armload onto a study table with a huff. "Stocked it with things from town." Cricket began digging in a box. She pulled out some kids' clothes which she handed to Frenchie. "There are baby wipes and things to help you get cleaned up. Y'all look like you need to get some sleep. Go on and get some rest. It's getting late now anyway. Y'all are safe here," she said with a smile. "Can I get you anything else?"

I eyed the table. She'd thought of everything. "No. Cricket …thank you."

Cricket smiled. "Gotta save the living, right?"

After they were gone, I turned back to my group. Everyone was looking expectantly at me. I glanced outside. We'd spent most of the night and day in the truck driving back to the college. From the looks of the sky, twilight was not far off. And Cricket was right, they all looked tired. Ethel could barely keep her eyes open, and poor Frenchie looked dead on her feet. God forbid we had to run again anytime soon.

"All right. Let's get some rest, but we'll set a watch and rotate shifts. Who is awake enough for first watch?" I asked.

"I can stay up," Will said.

I eyed him over. His movements showed me he was antsy, excited. I couldn't blame him. Cricket was very pretty. No wonder his mind was busy.

"All right, but stay put."

He nodded.

"Everyone else get some sleep. We can decide what to do next tomorrow."

"Mommy, I want to go home," Susan muttered tiredly, her face buried into her mother's leg.

Frenchie stroked her head but didn't say anything.

Everyone grabbed some blankets and wandered off, half collapsing into the small study rooms off the main floor of the library. I watched them all go. What were we going to do next? Their guess was as good as mine.

LAYLA

Jaime selected a room at the very back of the library. By the time I joined him, he'd already pushed the study table into the hallway and arranged some couch cushions on the floor. One blind was still open; he stood looking outside. I entered silently then went to Jaime and wrapped my arms around him, pressing my cheek against his back. He entwined his hands in mine then exhaled deeply. We stood in silence for several moments. I pulled away and came to stand at Jaime's side. He looked down at me, studying my face closely. His eyes were glossy as he fought back tears.

I reached up and touched his face.

He kissed my hand greedily, his tears wetting my fingers. Then he leaned in and kissed me passionately, pulling me close to him. He crushed me with such possessive desperation that I could barely breathe, but I did not resist. He kissed my face and neck, breathing deeply as he smelled my hair. The warmth of his skin felt good, and when he moved to unfasten my chest holster, I didn't stop him. Instead, I worked quickly to assist him. The guns hit the carpeted floor with a thud and moments later he was pulling my shirt over my head. My mind, at least the part of it still stuck in the past, called forth embarrassing misgivings about my physical appearance. You don't want your lover to see you naked for the first time with a week's worth of grime on your skin, gore crusted in your hair, and hands calloused and smelling like gun powder. Jaime didn't notice or care. He breathed heavily as he stroked my naked back. I slid his shirt off his shoulders and kissed his chest. Gently, he stroked my breasts with the back of his hands, gliding them across their curves. He then leaned in to kiss my breasts, his hands supporting the small of my back.

He got on his knees and kissed my stomach, moving down toward my belt buckle which he undid while his eyes made steady contact with mine. He wore a look on his face I'd never seen before; it was a strange mix of love, desperation, despair, and desire. His gaze moved me. He kissed my stomach gently, pressing his check against my belly as he pulled off my boots and slid my pants to the floor. Stepping away from the clothes, I kicked them aside.

Jaime removed the rest of his clothes. I felt that strange shyness mixed with passion that you sometimes feel when you make love to someone for the first time. I slid off my panties. Despite my initial nervousness, I had to remember this was Jaime. I loved Jaime. I was safe with him. There was no one in the world with a more honest heart than Jaime. As we pressed our naked bodies together, our sensitive skin touching one another, everything felt right.

Jaime whispered in my ear, "We're living on borrowed time. I can't stand the thought that one of us might die before…"

He didn't have to finish. "I know," I said then. "I know," I repeated, kissing him passionately.

Our bodies moved like we'd been together for years. We touched each other gently but with passion. I pressed my face against his neck. I smelled the sweet scent of his skin. When I kissed his neck, he tasted salty. I leaned against the wall, pulling Jaime toward me. We took our time, touching and feeling one another, but then the passion rose up in me, and I couldn't stand it any longer. Moments later, we were moving together. Our hearts were beating rhythmically as we made love. At some point, I realized I was crying. When I kissed Jaime, I found that he too was weeping.

"I love you," he whispered in my ear. "I love you so much."

"I love you too."

When it was over, we lay down together on the makeshift bed Jaime had fashioned for us. We held each other tightly. I momentarily allowed the fear and anguish to seep in and become a muddled mess with the euphoric feelings of love. Jaime slept while I cried. I wept first for the loss of my grandmother all those months ago. And then I wept for Ian. I wept for those from Hamletville who had died because of my own stupidity. And then I wept out of frustration. My mind felt like it was fracturing. How in the hell was I supposed to manage all of this? I was no one special. I snuggled closer to Jaime, pressing my head against his chest. Then I fell into exhausted sleep as I wept for a future that may never come.

CRICKET

Vella was waiting for me in the faculty lounge where she, Ariel, and I had settled in since arriving at Claddagh-Basel. She was looking out the window. She was so thin. Food was meager, but these days Vella wasn't really herself. She rarely ate or slept. She just spent her time studying her cards. Ariel was gone, as usual, probably floating around somewhere with Darius.

"I won't say I told you so," Vella said then, turning back to look at me. She smirked. I noticed then that her eyes looked a bit sunken.

"Okay, okay. It was just like you said, right down to the sword. But Vella, what does it mean? And second, when was the last time you ate somethin'?" For the last week, Vella's cards kept calling up the Queen of Swords over and over again. Vella had been getting strange headaches, and seeing the number 4 in her dreams and everywhere else. Finally, she came to Tristan and me with a map and a crazy theory that we needed to go on April 4th to Route 4 at 4 a.m. I was starting to think that Vella was starting to lose it when Tristan, who was right more often than Vella, convinced me otherwise. Surprising me, both Tristan and Doctor Gustav had agree to let me and Chase go looking for Vella's number four...but only after Vella told the doc "the two of swords will bring you what you seek." It hadn't made much sense to me at the time, but sure enough we found that truck with two swords. And inside, well, the doc had been looking for those meds for months. It unnerved me that I'd come back to Claddagh-Basel with both things Vella had foreseen. The last time her visions were so clear, the world had ended.

"How did she seem to you?" Vella asked.

"Who?"

"The Queen of Swords."

I frowned. I didn't like the nickname. "Rattled. Somethin' isn't sittin' right. There is more to the story, she's just not sayin' what. And you didn't answer my other question."

"There is suspicion in her eyes. But, whatever she is hiding, it isn't her we have to fear. And I'll eat something first thing tomorrow morning."

"You'd better. But this girl—and her name is Layla—how can you be so sure she's all right? We don't know her from Adam."

Vella shrugged. "Because the cards said so."

"We'll see what Tristan makes of her."

"She's not a threat. The cards say we need her."

I nodded. "You see Tristan?"

Vella shook her head. "He went to the woods early this morning. I am sure he'll be back soon...now that you're here, of course," she said then winked at me.

I hoped she was right. I hated when Tristan wandered off like that. He was going to be the death of me. "Get some rest. I'll be back later."

"It's nearly dark. Where are you headed?"

"Just for a look around," I replied, but I knew Vella would see through me.

"Check near the big oak in the back."

I grinned. "Thanks. Get some sleep. Maybe now your bad dreams will stop."

"Yes," Vella said, exhaling heavily. "I hope so."

I wound down the back stairwell and went outside through the west exit. It was twilight. Everything was calm and quiet. With the sound of cars gone and the bright lights of towns extinguished, nights were peaceful. I stared up at the sky. The first stars had just started twinkling. If the world hadn't been overrun with zombies, the end of humanity wouldn't have been such a bad thing. I had to admit, I'd been pretty lucky. Claddagh-Basel had been a haven. Ever since Tristan had brought us here, we'd been safe. We'd had a few run-ins with zombies, but we were able to handle everything that had been thrown at us. Sometimes I felt like we'd been protected. I hoped our luck stayed that way.

I walked toward the oak tree growing along the wall at the back of the campus green. When Tristan snuck off, this was always the route he used, climbing up the tree and over the wall. Of course, he couldn't just go through the front gate like everyone else. He had to be different. I sighed. If Tristan was still beyond the walls at this late hour I was going to have to choke him…if I didn't kiss him first.

Just as I was nearing the massive oak, which had grown half into the wall, Tristan swung down from an upper limb and jumped to the ground. He turned and looked my direction. "Cricket? Is that you?"

"What are you doing out there in the dark?" I scolded him.

"I have a flashlight," he said, smiling. He clicked the light on and off to prove his point. "I'm glad to see you're back. Vella's dream…did you—"

"We found a group of survivors and plucked them out of a horde of zombies. There was a girl with them, their leader. She was carrying a sword."

"And the two of swords?"

"We found the meds the doc was after."

Tristan was quiet for a moment. He took a deep breath then exhaled slowly, thoughtfully. "It's a beautiful night," he said then, reaching for my hand. "Shall we enjoy it together?

Typical Tristan, he was mysterious as ever. Though I tried to pry, he never said much about where he was from other than he'd been on his way to Claddagh-Basel when we crossed paths. Apparently he was associated with the college, a big donor or something. After Fairway Fun, he'd brought us to Claddagh-Basel. And ever since then, he stayed close to me. I'd spent all winter trying to get even closer to him, but he never made a move on me. He wanted me. I could see it in his eyes, but he held himself back and I wasn't sure why. It was frustrating as hell.

"All right," I replied, putting my hand in his.

"Your fingers are cold," he told me, then pulled me close to him, wrapping his arm around me.

I melted into him. His body was warm and soft. I could smell the sweet scent of the woods in his clothes. Tristan led us to the benches surrounding a small reflecting pool. The moon shone down on the water, making the pool sparkle with silver light.

"Beautiful," I whispered as I sat down on the bench.

Tristan joined me.

"As are you," he replied, pushing my strawberry-blonde hair over my shoulder.

"Flattery will get you everywhere," I said in a singsong then.

"Crick," he said with a laugh, gently touching my chin.

"Hard to remember there are zombies just outside on a beautiful night life this."

Tristan smiled sadly. "But there are. We have hibernated all winter, but so have they. Soon, they will start to move. And when they move…"

I gave Tristan a serious look. "What do you mean? You expect we'll see more of them soon?"

"It's spring. And, well," he said, then stopped. "Don't worry. I'll always be at your side."

"I don't like it when you and Vella start talkin' like you know somethin' I don't. If you do know somethin', isn't it about time you told me? How much longer are you going to wait? Pretty soon, I'm going to force it out of you."

"And how will you do that, lovely tilt girl."

"A lady does not divulge her methods."

"Then I shall look forward to your trying."

"Won't you just tell me? Tristan, what is it? I know you're keepin' a secret. What is it?"

Tristan looked down at me, a serious expression on his face. Under the light of the moon, he seemed to be surrounded by a silver glow. His eyes sparkled, reflecting the light in the pool. His dark hair framed his face handsomely.

"Tristan?" I whispered. Why in the hell wouldn't he just tell me, or kiss me, or something.

"Not tonight," he said then pulled me close to him. "But soon," he added, surprising me.

And while his words should have made me happy, knowing that whatever it was that he'd been keeping to himself was about to come out into the open, now I didn't feel so sure. Why now? Only one thing had changed. The Queen of Swords, as Vella called her, had arrived.

LAYLA

Sleepless, perhaps afraid to sleep, I stayed awake stewing over, well, everything. What should we do next? Ian was gone, as were so many others. Vampires were real. Zombies were trying to eat us alive. And I had been betrayed. The fox woman, whoever she was, had wanted us dead. She'd used us to kill the vampires then led us into a trap. Why? I stared out the window. It was dark, but I could still see people moving around on the grounds outside. They seemed so safe here. Maybe, just maybe, we could be safe here too. But how had we gotten here…from the HarpWind to Maryland? And just how had Cricket and Chase found us in the middle of the woods?

I sighed and lay down, curling up next to Jaime. What little sleep I managed to carve out was fitful, punctuated by nightmares. Strange images haunted my dreams. In one dream, I found myself in the kitchen of my grandmother's house. She was standing at the oven cooking dinner.

"You need to see, Layla," my grandmother told me in the dream, her back to me, "see the shadows and the light."

"Grandma?"

She turned then. Her eyes were moon-white, froth dripping from her chin. She hissed and lunged at me.

Flung from the dream, I bolted upright. My heart pounded in my chest. I was sweating. I tried to breathe deeply, forcing myself to inhale and exhale slowly as I shook off the dream.

Voices rose from outside. It was dawn. Dim sunlight shone through the window. I stood up, looked out. Through the thick morning mist, I spotted the silhouettes of Chase, Cricket, and a couple of other people. It looked like they were heading out.

I looked down at Jaime who was sleeping peacefully then back outside. Cricket was loading a pistol, a frustrated look on her face as she talked to Kellimore. I glanced again at Jaime. I couldn't bear to wake him, but I needed to get outside. I needed air. Still dressed, I grabbed my shashka and the Magnum, hoping someone would have ammo, and headed out.

In the library common area, I found Tom on watch. "Layla? You all right?" he asked, surprised to see me. He had been thumbing through a book. A quick glance of the spine told me he'd been reading one of Doyle's Sherlock Holmes classics.

"Some noise below. I'm going to check it out, see if I can lend a hand."

Tom looked pensive. "Where's Jaime? Someone should go along."

I shook my head. "I'll be all right. Let the others sleep. Just keep an eye on everyone? I'll be back in a bit."

Tom looked unsure, but he nodded. "Be careful."

"What's the worst that could happen?"

"Hellhounds?" Tom asked, lifting the book. He'd been reading *The Hound of the Baskervilles*.

"Nothing surprises me anymore."

Tom smiled weakly.

I headed into the dark hallway and carefully made my way to the stairs. I would need to ask Cricket for a flashlight. At the end of the hall, windows dimly illuminated the stairwell with predawn light. I had not noticed the night before, but a lovely stained glass image had been crafted on the window. I stopped to look at it. It depicted the Pieta, the Virgin Mary leaning over a dying Christ. Their faces looked long and narrow, distorted by the glass. The blue and red in the glass made blobs of colored light shimmer on the floor.

When I got to the first floor, I followed the exit signs to the main exit at the font of the college. As I walked, I passed only one person, a wisp of a little old man with enormous glasses. He barely looked at me as he scurried quickly down the hall. Voices rose from a room down the hall marked Student Union. There would be time for making acquaintances later. I needed to get some air.

I pushed open the door and walked down the driveway to join the group. While I couldn't see them well, the morning fog still thick, I could hear them. They were still arguing.

"No guns. Just go hand to hand," Kellimore was saying. From the sound of his voice, I sensed it wasn't the first time he'd suggested it.

"I'm not leaving my weapon here just because you said so," Chase answered, "whether I plan to use it or not."

"Stop fightin'. We'll just go check it out then—" Cricket was saying but stopped when she saw me.

All of them turned to look at me.

Taking a deep breath, I unsheathed the shashka. "Need a blade?"

Frowning, Kellimore looked me over. "Great, one of your newbies, Cricket."

"I'm Layla," I replied stiffly.

Ignoring Kellimore, Cricket turned to me. "We've been plannin' to make a run to the local school, but someone spotted a whole bunch of zombies on that end of town. We're going to go check it out, see how many there are."

"Once we stop arguing about nothing," Chase said, shooting Kellimore an exasperated look.

"I just don't think we should waste ammo," Kellimore said.

"Kellimore, we are just going on reconnaissance, not into battle," a tall, handsome stranger with dark hair and gold-colored eyes said then turned to me. "Welcome, Layla. I'm Tristan." Tristan eyed my blade then simply nodded his head ever-so-slightly in greeting.

From the moment he opened his mouth, Tristan caught my attention. His accent seemed both strange and familiar. No doubt my mind was just playing tricks on me, but Tristan seemed to have an odd glow about him. While I wasn't sure why, he seemed very familiar to me.

"Have I met you before?" I asked him.

Tristan smiled then shook his head. "No."

"You any good with that thing?" Kellimore asked, glancing at my shashka.

"I guess you'll find out."

"Where did you get it?" a young woman wearing baggy camouflage print pants, her hair boasting an undercut shave, asked. She took a long draw on her cigarette. The buckles on her combat boots clicked as she tapped them against the cobblestone driveway.

"It was mine...before."

"Really? Why?" she asked.

"I'm a historian. Well, I was. Ancient weapons were my specialty."

"It's all history now, isn't it," Cricket said with a laugh then added, "With Layla, we've got enough people. Let's go see what has them stirred up."

"Fine," Kellimore said with an exasperated huff. We turned and set off toward the gate.

"I'm Elle," the young woman said then, sticking out her free hand. "Don't mind Kellimore. He acts like a douche, but he's not that bad," Ella said then stopped to snuff out her cigarette. She stuck the butt in her pants pocket. "Tristan gets pissed if we litter," she explained. "The world has turned to ash, but he's still uptight about the environment."

"I heard that," Tristan said good-naturedly.

Elle laughed.

When we reached the gate, Kellimore consulted with the two men on guard.

"Don't get over-run. Just check it out then come back. No playing, Kellimore," an older man with a thick salt and pepper beard said as he pulled the gate open. The old wrought-iron gate opened with a screech that echoed down the valley. We headed out the gate and down the steep hill toward the main street of the college town. It suddenly occurred to me that I was on unfamiliar ground. If I got in a bind, I wouldn't know where to run. Perhaps that is the single most realistic reason why we'd survived in Hamletville. We knew our home court. Maybe it was a mistake to not go back.

Mist covered the road. I looked back at the college. It was shrouded in fog, but its tall towers sat above the murkiness, sunlight glinting off the roof tiles. I couldn't see more than twenty feet in front of me.

Cricket hummed an old Indigo Girls song under her breath as we headed down the hill away from the college. The tune brought forth embarrassing remembrances of steamy nights in the backseat of Ian's car. When we got to the bottom of the hill, we turned and followed Main Street. I tried to pay attention to all the street signs as we headed into town. In the thick fog, the place seemed eerie. The town must have dated to the Victorian era if not earlier. There were several large brick buildings and Victorian houses all along the street. Scarecrows, which had been tied to the parking meters, decorations for the Autumn Leaf Festival, had decayed in the winter weather. Their once-smiling faces sagged, their burlap clothing hanging in tatters. As we moved down the street, I realized the fog was thicker.

"Mist is rising off the lake," Kellimore said then, scanning all around.

It was eerily quiet. I thought about my grandmother. How many times had she warned me against wandering around in the fog?

Thin places, she would tell me. *Always be mindful of the thin places in our world. There, all things walk.*

Cricket was about to hum the chorus when Kellimore shushed her.

She stuck out her tongue at him.

He rolled his eyes then motioned for us all to stop. At first, I didn't hear anything. Then, through the echoing mist, I heard a sound like heavy breathing. Slowly moving down the street toward us, I spotted one of the undead. His body was severely decayed. His clothing hung in rags. Thin wisps of blond hair stuck out of his mottled skull. The sharp scent of decay wafted from him.

"Where'd he come from?" Elle whispered.

Kellimore shook his head. "Don't recognize him."

"Careful now. He may have friends," Cricket whispered.

Chase pulled out a knife but I also saw him pull his pistol and click off the safety.

Moving stealthily through the fog, Kellimore swept in on the undead man and bashed him on the side of the head with a baseball bat. Even after the first swipe, the undead man tried to lunge at him, but with a second strike, Kellimore sent brains splattering onto the street. The undead man fell over with a grunt.

"You see a lot of them?" Elle whispered to me.

I nodded. "We locked down our town, kept things safe for a while. But it was bad at first."

"I've been at the college the whole time. I was studying art. The Army evacuated a lot of people from this town, but the ones that were left...well, it was a battle. The college saved us."

"The castle, you mean," Tristan interrupted with a smile.

"Yes, yes," Elle replied. "We know. Brought over from Ireland—"

"Brick by brick," Chase added with a good-natured grin.

"Then reconstructed just as she had been in the old country," Tristan finished.

I saw Cricket look back at Tristan and smile, her expression warm and loving. Chase, who had been smiling, frowned and looked away.

"For the love of God, will you people shut up," Kellimore grumbled. "I can't hear a damned thing."

Elle rolled her eyes. "Bite me," she told him.

Kellimore frowned, but said nothing.

Quietly, we turned down Lakeside Drive. After walking for a few minutes, the lake finally came into view. The mist was just beginning to rise off the surface. I could smell the fresh scent of the water on the breeze. Thick cattails trimmed the shore. The sight and smells made me feel lonely for Hamletville.

As we walked up a small hill, I spotted a sign for the school: *Red Branch School, home of the dragons*. The sign was painted white with green trim. Two dragons, one red, one white, decorated the sign. On the side of the hill I could see the outline of a large building. It must have been the school.

Tristan motioned for us to stop. He tapped his ear, and we all listened.

Through the fog, we could hear the undead. I wasn't sure how close they were, but I knew one thing for sure, there were too many of them. I closed my eyes and tilted my head. I could hear...something. There was a soft sound like a whisper rattling through my mind, like a jumble of incoherent words. A moment later, the first of them appeared through the fog. A horde of more than two dozen decayed corpses moved toward us. At first, they seemed confused, lost. They were looking around as if they didn't know where they were. Seconds later, they spotted us. All at once, they turned toward us, their hungry mouths snapping.

LAYLA

7

"Run! This way," Kellimore yelled as he hustled down a path that led in the direction of the school. "Come on!"

"Here we go," Elle grumbled then unzipped her coat and pulled out two machetes.

Cricket gave Tristan a nervous look then twirled her enormous pipe wrench, and we all took off behind Kellimore. Chase brought up the rear.

We rushed down the path behind the bleachers. "This way," Kellimore called, hurrying to the gate that surrounded the football field. He opened the gate. "Go! We'll lure them in then lock them into the field."

"Can we get out?" I asked breathlessly as I rushed in behind him.

Kellimore nodded. "Scale the fence on the opposite side. I'll double back and lock them in. I'm always ready for Friday night lights," he said with a grin then took off.

The shambling undead rushed around the corner and filtered down the aisle toward the football field. Dammit. I hated not knowing where I was, and the mist hadn't lifted. The sun burned yellow, but fog was still heavy.

"Fan out and move backward," Chase said, motioning.

Kellimore ran down the sidelines, but a few undead broke from the pack and tried to follow him.

"Here," I called, trying to get their attention. "No, over here," I yelled.

The undead following Kellimore turned and rushed toward me. The only problem was that they weren't the only ones who heard me. All at once, the entire horde seemed to see only me.

I gasped and pulled out my shashka.

"Layla, look out," Cricked yelled.

"Head to the fence," Elle called. "Layla, come on!"

I glanced back to see Cricket grab Elle by the back of her jacket, and they headed across the field.

"Move," Chase yelled at me.

I turned and ran with the others toward the far side of the field.

Soon, the fence came into view. We were fast, but not fast enough. As we reached the fence, the first few of the undead reached us.

"Go," I yelled to Cricket, then I let my blade do her work. I paused and waited as the first of the undead rushed me. Running with a limp, a hungry looking woman with stringy red hair and a tattered dress practically threw herself at me. Stretching out my arms, I sliced her in half. Her legs rushed forward several steps while her torso slid sideways to the ground. When her legs finally dropped, a heap of bloody guts emptied onto the earth. Her upper body lay on the ground nearby. She snapped at me, her eyes milk-white and bloody.

I quickly stabbed her through the head then turned with a fast spin to decapitate the next undead man rushing me. His head flew into the air, a shadow in the fog against the early morning sunrise.

Beside me, I saw Elle's blades flash as she stabbed and slashed. She made short work of the undead man who tried to attack her.

"Layla, Elle, come on," Chase yelled as he boosted Cricket up and over the fence then scrambled up behind her.

The other undead were advancing but more slowly. I could see them lumbering toward us in the mist. I turned to

Elle who nodded to me. We ran to the fence where Tristan was waiting.

Elle slid her blades back into their scabbards then climbed up and over the fence.

I sheathed my shashka and Tristan and I followed.

"Safe! They're locked in," Kellimore yelled from the other side of the field.

I moved quickly over the fence. I climbed down then jumped to the ground. Chase reached out to steady me. Tristan landed on the ground beside me with a thud.

"We need to check the fence, sweep it. We need to make sure they can't get out," I said between breaths. My lungs burned.

Cricket nodded. "This way," she said.

We rounded the fence. The undead, at least two dozen of them, were trapped inside. They followed our steps but could not keep pace with us. The fence was intact. Soon we were at the gated entrance between the school and the field. The gate was padlocked. When the undead reached the fence, they slammed into it in a frustrated jumble. Their mouths open, they snapped and bit at us. I could almost feel their terrible hunger.

"I don't think I moved that fast at the homecoming game," Kellimore said, joining us.

"Hustle when it counts," Chase said, clapping Kellimore on the shoulder.

Kellimore's dark hair was wet with sweat, his blue eyes flashing. In that moment, I saw a glimmer of something behind his eyes. He was sad. Being on that field again had reminded him of something he'd lost…his life, his future, his dreams. In that moment, I pitied him.

"You did great," I told him. "Smart thinking."

He shrugged, and once again he pulled the mask back on. "Just like herding cats. Now we can pick them off like flies," he said, and to prove his point, he pulled a long hunting knife from his belt and stabbed an undead man through the head.

Following suit, we made short work of the undead crowding the fence. Their lifeless bodies heaped all around the gate.

Elle pulled out a crumpled cigarette. She offered one to me, but I shook my head.

"I didn't smoke either, not until this shit started," she said, motioning to the dead bodies.

"Bad time to pick up a soon-to-be extinct habit," I told her with a grin.

"Well, we're a soon-to-be extinct species, so I guess it hardly matters," she said with a laugh, then inhaled deeply.

"Where are we supposed to find this thing the doc is looking for again?" Cricket asked, pulling a piece of paper out of her pocket.

"Chemistry lab," Kellimore replied, taking the paper from her hand.

I looked over to see that Kellimore was holding a magazine cutout of a small centrifuge machine.

"Is the building clear?" I asked, looking up at the large school building. It was three stories in height and made of brick.

Kellimore nodded. "We cleared it out early on, took all the food and medicine over to the college."

"Yeah, but still, go slow," Elle said. "Better safe than sorry."

Kellimore nodded. "Let's go around front. The chem lab is facing Laurel Street. Door is close on that side." He turned and trotted up the steps toward the front of the building. We followed behind.

When we got to the top of the stairs, I paused and looked out across the football field. The mist had finally thinned. It shimmered golden. I caught a glimpse of the lake. The reflected sunlight made me wince as it danced with a million golden sparkles on the waves. I sheltered my eyes with my hand and looked back toward the football field. Then, I saw someone standing in the field. Someone was walking slowly toward us, toward the heap of zombies. My heart leapt into my throat. It was daytime, so it couldn't be a vampire, but still, something about the way it moved seemed odd.

Slowly, I stepped back down the stairs. An undead man crossed the field toward me. He was clearly dead, his eyes were the same milky white as the others, but he didn't snap and snarl. He kept his chin low on his chest and seemed to stare at me. His clothing hung in a tattered mess, but I could see that he was wearing scrubs. His feet were bare. His skin was deathly pale but not decayed as the others had been.

I twirled the shashka in my hand and approached the fence, ready to strike him down as I had the others.

"Stop," I heard a male voice whisper in my head. The undead man tilted his head and looked at me.

My heart pounded in my chest.

Stepping on the corpses, he came forward and linked his fingers in the fence. He stood staring at me. Unlike the others, he was not in attack mode. His stillness allowed me to see him more clearly. I could see he had a large bite mark on his shoulder. His worn, teal-colored scrubs were stained red at the wound.

"Can you hear me?" I whispered in a barely audible voice.

He made a deep, exhaling sound that seemed to rattle from his chest, but he was not breathing. It almost seemed like he was trying to control…what, his rage? His hunger? I didn't know.

"Help us," he whispered inside my head.

Before I could reply, he turned his attention toward the stairs and snarled.

A gun blasted, and the undead man in front of me stilled. His fingers clutched the fence for a moment and then he crumbled onto the heap of corpses lying at the gate, a bullet hole in his forehead.

I looked back to see Chase at the top of the stairs, gun in his hand. "You okay, Layla? Christ, he looked like he was about to scale the fence."

"I'm all right. Just froze," I replied.

Chase nodded then headed back.

I froze because I'd heard him. I had heard him, and he'd asked me for help. I stared down at him. He looked different from the others. The others looked more decayed, more like rotting corpses. This creature looked undead, but not decaying, at least, not at the same rate. Maybe he'd been locked up somewhere. Or maybe...well, I didn't know what. Maybe I was losing my damned mind.

Shaking, I took a deep breath and turned to follow the others only to find Tristan standing behind me. He was staring at the undead man. After a moment, he shifted his gaze and looked at me, his eyes meeting mine. He inclined his head toward me, and we turned and followed the others inside.

LAYLA

Kellimore slid the chain from the locked door and opened it slowly. The metal door opened with a squeak.

"Hello?" he called into the darkened hallways. His voice echoed through the building, startling a flock of crows that cawed then flew off the roof.

We waited a few moments, everyone straining to listen for, well, anything.

A soft breeze made the metal hook on the flag pole in front of the school clap. The flag hung in tatters. Its red, white, and blue were deeply faded, the ends of the flag frayed.

"Clear," Kellimore said.

"I'll stand guard," Elle said, then took a position on the steps at the front of the school.

Stepping slowly, we followed Kellimore inside. The hall was dimly lit, light streaming in from the dirty classroom windows. The walls had been painted gray-blue, the floor tiles matching. Children's artwork hung on the bulletin boards in the hallway. Construction paper jack-o-lanterns, yarn scarecrows, and leaf rubbings decorated the place. On the billboard of the first grade room across the hall, the teacher had made a large construction paper oak tree with small acorns on the ground below. On each acorn someone had written a child's name. *Watch how we grow*, the sign read. It wounded me to think most of the children were probably dead. I inhaled deeply and tried not to think about it.

"In here," Kellimore said, then led us to a door marked "Chemistry Lab." He, Cricket, and Chase went inside and I heard them discussing—well, more like bickering—once they were in the room.

Tristan waited with me in the hallway. There was an uncomfortable silence. Had he heard me? Had he heard the man? Christ, had I really heard the man? What was going on? Trying to break the silence, I asked, "Are you from here?"

"No, I was travelling with Cricket."

"But...but you knew about the college?"

"I've been connected to the college for many years. I was not far from here when things went bad. I knew the college would be safe, so I helped Cricket and the others reach here in one piece."

"Connected to the college? How? Did you teach here?"

Tristan raised a dark eyebrow at me. Apparently my prying wasn't coming off as conversational as I hoped. "No, but I liked to come here from time to time to share my gifts," he finally replied. "We all have our gifts, don't we?"

It was my turn to raise an eyebrow at him. Did he know?

Tristan smiled gently.

My instincts had failed me. I studied Tristan's face, knowing there was something more to him, but I didn't know what. And whatever he was, I had no idea if I could trust him or not. "Yes, we do," I said simply. I then crossed the hall to the first grade room. Turning the knob slowly, I opened the door. "Hello?" I called.

"Can I help you?" Tristan asked.

"No, I'll be just a minute," I said then went inside. The school reminded me a lot of our local school in Hamletville, every grade packed into one building. I glanced around the classroom. Each child's seat had been lovingly decorated with a name plaque, and a bucket of crayons and markers sat at the center of each table.

Some backpacks lay forgotten in the cubbies. I grabbed a pink backpack, decorated with the last Disney princess, and emptied the contents: a water bottle, mittens, and an empty lunchbox. I then went to the teacher's desk and grabbed books from the desk, loading readers, math books, science books, anything she had lying around into the backpack. I then stuffed the bag with all the crayons, markers, paper, and stickers I could fit inside. Against all hope, I prayed that giving Kira and Susan something normal to occupy their minds would help.

Cricket stuck her head inside. "We got it. You all right?"

"Yeah, just grabbing some things."

"You've got those little girls with you. Was that their mama, the redhead?"

I nodded. "Frenchie."

"Dad make it too?"

I shook my head. "Long gone, before."

"Well, at least they've got their mama. If you're ready, we can go."

I slung the backpack over my shoulder, and we headed outside.

"I never saw that movie," Cricket said, motioning to the backpack. "Don't suppose I'll ever see a movie again."

"Or watch another Steelers game," Kellimore said.

"Or eat another Big Mac," Elle added.

"But now there is quiet, and space, and—" Tristan began wistfully.

"And the undead," I finished.

Cricket sighed. "Without them, might be nice to reboot things."

"That's the problem," Kellimore said. "Without them. There is no without them now."

"Aren't they all going to rot? I mean, how long can a dead body just walk around?" Cricket asked.

"I've noticed they don't all look so rotten? Why is that?" Elle asked.

"Could be they were locked up inside somewhere," Chase mused.

"Maybe," Tristan said then looked at me.

I didn't say a word.

LAYLA

"Doc's lab is down this way," Cricket said as we wound down the dark hallway in the unused wing of the building. The others had dispersed when we returned, leaving Cricket and me to deliver the supplies.

"It's so quiet," I said.

"Yeah, she doesn't like much noise, or company, or smilin'," Cricket said with a laugh. "But, she's trying to figure out what happened. I suppose you need quiet to think about things like that."

As we neared the doctor's lab, I was surprised to hear a male voice join the doctor's.

Quietly, Cricket knocked on the door.

"Come in," Doctor Gustav called.

"We're back," Cricket said as we entered.

"Did you find it?"

"Sure did, and the other things you wanted."

I entered quietly behind Cricket. The doctor's lab looked like it had been some sort of classroom. She had transformed the place, however, into a full blown laboratory. On every desk she had papers, bottles, and brewing concoctions. It looked like something from a movie. There were some small rooms off the main lab. They had been marked "Do not enter. Keep free of contaminants." On one wall, the doctor had small cages with rats inside. Thus far, I hadn't seen any animal contaminated with whatever it was that had killed mankind. The rats looked perfectly normal, at least on the outside.

"Layla?" a voice called. I spotted Jaime crossing the room carrying an armload of equipment.

"Jaime. How'd you end up down here?"

"I was worried, went looking for you. Tom said you went out with the others, but I got turned around in the halls and ended up here."

"Which was a good thing," Doctor Gustav said then. "Jaime tells me he's a medic. I've been looking for an extra hand."

"An extra hand for what?" I asked.

"Weird science," a voice answered from the doorway.

I looked back to see Tristan standing there, a harsh look of disapproval on his face.

"Tristan," the doctor said, looking at him over her glasses. Her lips pulled on both sides in either a smile or a grimace. I wasn't sure which. "The world has ended yet still I get to enjoy the oversight of a representative of this college's Board of Trustees. How can I help you?"

"I'm just here for Cricket," he said, ignoring her sharp retort. He turned his attention to the strawberry-blonde who smiled at him. "Want lunch?" he asked her.

"You cookin'?"

"Anything you like: sardines, shredded coconut flakes, animal crackers, it's all yours."

Cricket smiled. "Can I do anything else for you, doc?"

Doctor Gustav shook her head. "No, thank you, Cricket. And Tristan, thank you too. I understand you went out this morning as well?"

"To keep everyone safe. If you need something in the future, doctor, perhaps you can let me know before we send out another group? We came across a very large horde today. They seem to be on the move again. We don't want anyone getting hurt just looking for—"

"Yes, I know, gadgets for my weird science," the doctor said curtly. "Very well."

"Thanks for your help," Cricket told me with a wave then she and Tristan left Jaime and me alone with the doctor.

The doctor frowned as she dug into the pack Cricket had brought. "Ah. Here it is. What was I saying? Oh, yes. I've been in need of assistance for a while. I needed someone trained in medicine."

"Doctor Gustav is running some experiments. She's trying to pinpoint what caused the outbreak," Jaime told me.

I noticed then that the box Cricket had found in the truck was sitting on a table nearby. Several vials had been removed from the case. "What are those?" I asked.

"Flu vaccine," the doctor replied. "Weird science," she said with a scoff. "Tristan, well, he doesn't quite understand. I believe that the flu vaccine distributed in the fall may have played a part in the outbreak. I'm still doing tests, but it's so much work. I'm starting to see something. It's beyond luck that we recovered this box. Most of the vaccines were exposed to the weather, but by the grace of God, it appears two vials still contain a properly stored vaccination."

"You think the flu shot did this?" I asked aghast. My mind rattled back in time and I remembered my grandmother and me arguing for the ten-thousandth time about the flu shot.

"I will not put germs in my body to keep the germs out," Grandma Petrovich told me.

"But, Grandma, it will boost your immunity and protect your from known strains of the flu. And the vaccine is dead. It's not a live virus."

"Layla, have you grown a beard?"

I sighed. "No, Grandma, why?"

"Because you're talking like a philosopher. Little things make a big difference, my girl," she would say, and that would be the end of it.

"No," the doctor replied, interrupting my memories. "But it may have played a part."

"How?" Jaime asked.

"I believe it caused a reaction."

"To what?" Jaime asked.

"That's what I could use your help discovering," she told him.

Jaime smiled. He liked to help people. Maybe the work would take his mind off Ian. This match was probably a good thing. But just when I convinced myself to encourage him, I felt a chill. It wasn't something I felt against my skin, but more like something I felt in my mind. Great, now I was sensing the rats. I felt like my instincts had gone haywire.

"Shall I leave you to it then?" I asked Jaime. "I was going to take this bag upstairs to the girls. I grabbed them some books, crayons —"

"You don't need me?"

"Every day, with all my heart," I said with a smile, not caring what the doctor thought.

Jaime smiled then led me to the door. "You sure you'll be okay?" he asked. He reached out and stroked my cheek then planted a soft kiss on my lips. The sweet memory of our night together flashed back to mind.

"I'll find you later. Looks like she needs you," I said.

Jaime nodded. "Love you," he whispered in my ear.

"I love you too."

Then I turned and headed back down the dark hallway, realizing once more I still hadn't asked Cricket for a flashlight.

10

CRICKET

"There you go being protective again," I said playfully to Tristan as we made our way out the back door nearest the doctor's lab.

"I just don't like her putting you, or anyone else, in harm's way so she can advance her work," Tristan replied.

"She is tryin' to help," I reminded him. "You don't have to come next time. I got my wrench, and I know how to use it." I knew the idea of me going off alone would get under his skin, and I said it just to provoke a reply. This time, however, he surprised me.

"Cricket," he said, then stopped and wrapped his hands around my waist.

He looked deeply into my eyes, and I saw that same desperate want I'd seen there at least a hundred times before.

So why didn't he ever let himself just take what he wanted? Lord knows, I was ready to give it ninety-eight of those one-hundred times. The other two times I had a headache.

I took a step back and leaned against the wall. I wrapped my arms around his neck and pulled him toward me. When our lips touched, I felt like I'd been zapped by electricity.

Tristan pulled me close. He kissed me hard, passionately. He pressed my body against his, his hand stroking my back and down to my ass, feeling the soft curves of my body. I could feel him, his dick hard inside his pants. He wanted me, and I wanted him. I didn't see what the problem was.

I kissed his neck and whispered in his ear. "Tristan." I moved my hands under his shirt and felt his soft skin and hard muscles.

"I want you so badly," he whispered in my ear, "but I just can't." He pulled back.

My blood pumping through my veins, I could barely compose myself. "And why not?" I demanded. "Are you playing games with me?"

"No, Cricket, I love you," he replied.

"You love me?"

"Yes. More than anything in this dying world."

"Then what's holding you back? I want you," I said, feeling frustrated when tears started blurring my eyes. And men say women are complicated! I'd never met a more complicated man in all my life. Served me right for letting myself have feelings for someone. I'd cut Chase loose, hurt him in the process, just for Tristan. And all for what? A big fat nothing.

"There are things I can't explain to you, not yet. You just have to trust me."

"Yeah, I've about had it with that. All the time, trust me, trust me. Why? Why should I trust you? 'Cause you say you love me? Well, I love you too, but here we are. You want me," I said, motioning to his obvious erection, "and I want you. I don't understand. Were you married? Were you a priest? You got an STD? What? What is it? I just don't know how much more of this I can take. I do love you, but I don't like games."

"None of those things," Tristan replied in frustration. "I promise you."

"Well," I said then, as I adjusted my clothes and got my head on straight, "you better make your mind up real fast then, 'cause I've had it. I might be dead tomorrow, and the man I love has no good reason for not being with me. We don't have time, don't you understand? We're not going to live through this. Sooner or later, one of us is going be dead. We've just been lucky so far. And when that happens, there will be nothin' left but regret," I said angrily. Tears streamed down my cheeks. "Now, if you'll excuse me," I said, then turned and marched away from him.

"Cricket," he called.

I didn't answer him.

"Cricket, I'll make it right. I'm sorry. I'll make it right."

"Make up your mind," I called in reply then headed around to the front of the college.

Still fuming, my eyes wet with tears, I damned near smashed into Mister Iago as he was coming down the sidewalk pulling a massive wooden crate on wheels behind him. I caught myself just before I stumbled into the small man. My skin crawled at the thought of it. I couldn't believe my eyes when we arrived at Claddagh-Basel to find Mister Iago had, by chance, found his way there too. Of all the people from the carnival I'd hoped had made it out alive, he was last on the list.

"Cricket," he said aghast, "you all right?"

"Sorry, just lost my step," I said, then eyed the box. It was latched on the sides and was about six feet tall. "What is that?"

Mister Iago shifted uncomfortably. "Just something the doctor asked for."

Ugh! I was sick of men and their secrets. Without another word, I huffed around him then headed across the campus green to the small grotto near the gazebo and reflecting pool. Intended as a quiet place for the students to study, I couldn't think of a better place to go to hide from everyone and everything.

I slipped down the brush-lined path until I spotted the little cement pool. All around it grew daffodils. The yellow flowers perfumed the wind. In the grotto nearby, a statue of Saint Columba—at least that's who they told me it was—stood on a pedestal. I lay down on the grass and looked up at the sky. My head hurt. I lay there like that for I don't know how long when I heard someone approach. At first I was worried it was Tristan, back for another round of arguing, but as soon as she got close, I knew it was Vella.

"How'd the run go?" she asked.

"Whole bunch of zombies roamin' around town."

"Where'd they come from?"

"You tell me."

"I saw Layla go out with you. How was she?"

"Kick-ass. Girl is good with the sword."

"Your eyes are red."

"I suppose they are."

Vella sighed. "Fighting with Tristan again?"

"My own fault. I should have known better, should have kept my heart locked up right where it was. I could have been bouncin' on Chase's lap every night all winter instead of chasin' after Tristan. And, for what? A whole lot of nothin'."

Vella laughed. "There is still time, if you've changed your mind. Chase still—"

"Can't do that to him."

"Then what are you going to do?"

"I don't know. How about you pull me a card and tell me what to do."

"I think you should be patient with Tristan."

I cracked an eye open and looked at her. "And why do you think that?" I always had the sneaking suspicion that Vella knew something about Tristan I didn't. Not that she would tell me. They were both frustrating as hell.

"Because he's worth it."

"Right about now I could use one of your blue lights or stars or somethin' to show me what to do."

"Don't worry. I suspect it won't be long now."

"Long? Until what?"

Vella reached her hand out to me. "Come on, let's go eat something."

I took her hand, and rose, but when I did, I spotted Tristan in the distance moving toward the big tree at the back of the college.

"There he goes again," I said.

Vella turned to look.

"Where do you suppose he's goin'?"

"To sort things out."

"He told me he's going to make it right. What do you suppose that means?"

Vella pursed her lips then smiled. "Well, one way or another, we'll find out," she said then turned and headed back toward the building. "You coming?"

I watched as Tristan shimmied up the tree then dropped over the wall. My heart beat faster. Where was he going again? I flashed my eyes at the little white saint sitting in the grotto nearby then said a little prayer. *Bring him back safe.* Light shone down on the small statue and for a moment, it looked like Saint Columba was smiling.

"Yeah. Let's go. I'm hungrier than I thought."

LAYLA

"Layla? You all right? Summer and Tom went downstairs this morning to get some water and they said a group ran into some zombies in town," Ethel said in a rush when I entered the library.

I scanned the room quickly. All the Hamletville people were there. I breathed a sigh of relief then nodded. "We made a run for supplies, but we came across a horde. Got them taken care of. Otherwise, it's pretty quiet out there. The town is a lot like Hamletville, really. I have a surprise for my two special girls." I held out the backpack to Kira and Susan.

"What is that?" Kira called excitedly.

"Thank you, Layla," Susan exclaimed.

Frenchie stood over the girls and watched as they dug with wild excitement through the bag, pulling out the markers, crayons, stickers, and everything else.

"There are some school books in there," I told Frenchie. "I don't know how long we'll be here, but I thought it might distract them if they study."

Frenchie, who'd pulled her long red hair into a braid, smiled at me. "And me too. Thank you, Layla."

Summer stroked her hand across the spines of books on the shelf nearest her. "Look at this place. We're surrounded by so much wisdom, but nothing here can save us."

"Maybe, maybe not. Jaime met with Doctor Gustav this morning. She's working on pinpointing the cause of the contamination. She's getting close. Jaime is going to help her."

"Doctor Ice Princess," Tom said. "She warm up any?"

I smiled at him. "Not much."

"I'll go offer my help too," Kiki said. "Maybe she needs a hand with some equipment or something."

"That woman we saw in the hallway yesterday, the one with long, dark hair, just came by to say we should come eat. I don't know about you all, but I'm starving. Animal crackers can only hold a man my size for so long," Tom said.

I nodded. "Then let's go. Time to check the place out," I told them.

Everyone got ready, and soon we headed back downstairs. As we worked down the narrow hallways of the college, passing classrooms and offices, I realized that most of the spaces had been turned into living quarters. One open classroom door revealed mats on the floor and a clothesline strung across the room. Inside, a woman was nagging two teenage boys to tidy up their beds. People were coming and going, but they gave us a wide berth. The others looked much like our group; regular men and women, old and young, all worn thin by despair. Curious, people peered out through classroom doors as we passed by. Perhaps they expected the dregs of society to arrive at any moment, to torture, maim, and murder them. That was, after all, what the movies had taught us to expect.

The Student Union was a hubbub of activity and noise. There were more than thirty people inside socializing and eating lunch from paper plates. The room, however, fell silent when we appeared at the door.

"Well, this is awkward," Will said under his breath.

To our luck, Cricket and Elle were there.

"Layla," Cricket called. "Come in! We've got more applesauce than a person could dream of."

"Mommy, I'm hungry," Susan said shyly.

"Let's go," I said, motioning the others inside.

Cricket's warm welcome had broken the tension in the room. The others went back to eating, drinking, and playing cards.

"Layla, this is Vella," Cricket said then, introducing me to the dark-haired woman I'd seen when we first arrived.

"Nice to meet you," I told her. "Where are you from?" I asked. "I noticed your accent." Usually I wasn't so blunt, but the encounter with Rumor left me on edge, and there was something about Vella that was triggering my senses. I just wasn't sure what it was about her that had sparked my attention.

"I'm Romanian."

"You started without us," a voice said from behind me.

At first I thought it was Chase, but I turned to see another young man standing there. He was tall, his head shaved clean. Beside him was a girl about Kiki's age with long, dark hair.

"This is Darius and Ariel," Cricket introduced. "And this is Layla, the girl Chase and I plucked out of the woods."

"Hey," Ariel said and then smiled.

"Nice to meet you. Where's Chase?" Darius asked.

Cricket shrugged. "He and Kellimore were chewing Joe's ear off down at the gate. We ran into some zombies today."

"We just heard. Everyone okay?" Darius asked.

Cricket nodded.

"Where did they come from? We haven't seen any zombies for months," Ariel said with a frown.

Vella pulled out a deck of cards from her bag and started shuffling. She seemed distracted and was muttering to herself under her breath. Cricket cast a sidelong glance at her but didn't say anything.

"Don't know," Cricket said.

"It seemed like they just walked out of the mist," I added.

At that, Vella stopped and turned and looked at me.

"Yeah, it can get real foggy here in the mornings. Can't see anything until the afternoon some days," Cricket said with a frown.

"I'm starving," Ariel told Darius. "Nice to meet you," she told me then headed over to grab some food.

Vella frowned then looked away and went back to shuffling her cards.

I scanned the room. The Hamletville people had collected at one table. Some of the college people were stopping by to say hello. I sighed with relief. A warm, human welcome was a refreshing change.

"I won't keep you more," Cricket told me but then got distracted again by a newcomer.

"Pardon me," a little voice said from behind me. I turned around to see the little man with the big glasses I'd spotted earlier.

"Mister Iago, this is Layla," Cricket told him.

The little man looked up at me. His glasses looked like they hadn't been cleaned in a year. Flecks of white skin dirtied the lenses. I tried to hide the repulsion I felt. The repulsion, however, wasn't coming from the man's appearance but from my instincts. Something about the little man was just...wrong.

"Ma'am," he said then skirted by me.

"I...I better go check on my people," I said then, nodding to Cricket and Vella. "Nice to meet you," I told Vella then joined my group.

"Have you heard any news? Anything from the outside?" a woman was asking Ethel and Summer when I arrived.

"No, hun, we sure haven't," Ethel replied.

Several of the college people had come to the table and were asking questions. I said nothing but sat and listened. The group stuck as close to the truth as possible, one following the other's lead. We were all so spent, so exhausted, that we'd never thought about ensuring our group had a cohesive tale to tell. What they came up with on the spot, however, made sense. Outsiders came to Hamletville. We left with them and travelled to the HarpWind Grand Hotel. Someone got infected. The place was destroyed, and we were on the run. It sounded believable enough.

We lingered awhile. Finally seeing everyone was comfortable, I got up and fixed myself a plate of food:

sardines, circus peanuts, and some kind of jerky. Someone had set a bottle of superfood vitamins at the end of the table. I opened the bottle and sniffed it.

"They taste gross, but you'll get used to it. Try to take one a day. We got cases of them when we cleaned out the health food store downtown," Elle said as she forked a few sardines onto her plate. "Speaking of gross," she added as the fishy oil dripped down her hand.

I chuckled. It was spring. We'd planned to start planting early in Hamletville so we'd be ready for the next winter. We didn't want to depend on the dead world's leftovers. Now, I didn't know what was going to happen. I shook myself from my thoughts.

"Come meet my friends?" I offered Elle.

Nodding, she followed me back to the table and I introduced her around.

"What were you studying here?" Ethel asked.

"Graphic arts. I wanted to do web design. It's weird, isn't it? So much of our life existed in a virtual world. Now that world is gone, and most of my art with it," Elle replied.

"Do you know how to paint?" Kira asked.

Elle softened, pulled from the dark thoughts that had clouded her face. "I do."

"We love painting. Do you know how to make a 3-D house? We were learning that in kindergarten before everyone got sick," Kira said.

Elle nodded.

"Oh, will you teach us?" Susan asked.

"Please!" Kira added.

Elle smiled. "Only if you eat all your lunch," she said with a wink to Frenchie.

Kira and Susan stared at their plates, the sardines still untouched, then looked at one another. With a nod, they agreed. Forcing themselves, they ate the oily fish, grimacing all the while.

We laughed.

The rest of the day passed surprisingly quietly. As night drew near, however, I began to worry. Not only were the undead out there, but so were the fiends of the night. Was Rumor's group the only group of vampires or were there more? Could they follow us here? And more so, what about the fox woman? She knew, at least roughly, where we were. It may have taken us a day's ride to reach the college, but something told me that we were not yet out of the fox woman's reach. And if we had to run, where would we go?

Jaime joined me in bed just as I was drifting off to sleep later that night. He wrapped his arms around me and pulled me close.

"How is the work going?" I whispered sleepily.

"She's brilliant. She's won awards for her studies. She really is on to something. Kiki was down helping us too. It feels good to be useful," he said, burying his face in my hair.

"I hope we can make a go of it here," I said sleepily. I could feel my dreams starting to insist themselves upon me.

"It may be a fresh start. We might even find a cure."

"What a great dream."

"What else is left?"

He was right. Without hope, there was nothing.

LAYLA

I woke the next morning with a plan. Jaime had already gone back to work, but Buddie and Will were in the library looking out the window down over the campus green.

"Anyone up for a walk?" I asked.

"You read my mind," Buddie replied.

I grinned. "Shall we see if they'll let us out the gate?"

"After you," Buddie replied, motioning to the door.

We let Tom know we were heading out, then armed up.

While it was a good idea to get the lay of the land so we weren't running blind in a pinch, I had another reason for wanting to go outside the walls again. The undead man on the football field had spoken to me. This was the second time I'd clearly heard the undead speak. The undead man Rumor had chained to her bed had tried to communicate with me too. I needed to figure out what I was hearing. I needed to get close to one again, and that wasn't going to happen behind castle walls.

When we reached the gate, we found Kellimore there chatting with the guards.

"Man, you should have seen me. Layla was there, she saw. I must have booked downfield faster than I did during the game against the Hornets. You remember that, Joe?" Kellimore was saying.

The older man smiled at him. "I think the recruiter was at that game, wasn't he?"

Kellimore nodded. "He practically gave me the scholarship that night. What a game," he said, drifting a bit at the end, lost in his memories.

"What can we do for you...Layla, right?" the man Kellimore referred to as Joe asked.

I nodded. "These are my friends, Buddie and Will. We were wondering if we could go out for a look around. If we get pinned down, we don't know where we are. Just wanted to get a better feel of the area."

Joe looked at the other guard who nodded. Then he said, "People don't go outside the gate much. We try not to draw attention to the fact we're here."

"I'll go with them," Kellimore offered. "Give the tour."

Joe, who looked like he was feeling mildly relieved to get out of the conversation with Kellimore, nodded. Carefully, he unbarred the gate. The metal gate opened with a screech. "Watch yourselves."

"What's the worst that could happen?" Kellimore asked with a laugh.

Buddie, Will, and I all exchanged glances. We'd hate to be the ones to tell him.

Since it was approaching noon, the fog had started burning off and visibility was clear. We headed down the hill toward Main Street. The place was eerily quiet. All you could hear was the wind and, somewhere in the distance, the sound of a broken sign clattering. The button-eyed scarecrows frowned at us, watching in silent vigil. Weeds were growing all along the cracks in the sidewalk and street. The shop windows were dusty. Some cars, dirty and rusted from sitting out all winter, sat parked.

"Any of these vehicles run?" Will asked.

Kellimore shook his head. "We pulled their batteries, siphoned the gas. But, you see that car wash over there?" he asked, pointing.

On the corner was a car wash, its wash bays shuttered.

"There's an RV and a van locked up in there. Gassed and stocked. Ready in case we need a quick getaway."

"Locked though," Buddie observed.

"Doc's got the keys. And Tristan. We're not going anywhere without them," Kellimore said then motioned down the street toward the lake. "The lake's at the middle of the town. All the roads go in a circle around it except the four main roads in and out of town: Main Street, North Street, Lakeside Drive, and Red Branch Way."

I tried to envision the layout of the town in my head: it was a giant sun cross. "How old is this place? The college...the building was brought over from Ireland?"

Kellimore nodded. "The town was founded by the Irish long back. It was one of the first towns built in colonial times. Later, just like you said, they brought over the castle. I used to belong to the Sons of Red Branch. SRB was a lot like boy scouts, but they taught us about the old country too. A lot of those skills have come in handy," he said then led us down Main Street. "There's a small museum there," Kellimore said, pointing to a little stone building. "We pulled a ton of old stuff from there and ended up using it. I spent an entire afternoon this winter using a mortar and pestle to grind walnuts," he said then laughed. "As for the stores, we cleaned those out early on and locked everything up. We haven't had much trouble with looters. Some people passed through in the winter, but they never even knew we were at the college. They just stole some winter clothes and kept going. But we've heard stories."

"What kind of stories?" Will asked.

"Cricket and her group ran into some really bad characters…killed some of the people they were with. There are a lot of sick people running around out there."

While I was sure he was right, what had found us was much worse.

Buddie took notes on a small notepad as we followed Kellimore down Main Street then onto Solar Way, one of the streets that circled the lake.

"Hey, let's stop here a sec," Kellimore motioning to a small shop. The sign on the roof of the building read *Mrs. Lavender's Herbs and All-Natural Supplies*. "Doc asked me to grab some things next time I passed by."

We followed Kellimore onto the deck of the quaint little shop. Rocking chairs lined the porch. Mildewed bales of hay, rotted pumpkins and gourds, and dead mums sat beside the front door.

Kellimore pulled out a board that had been lodged through the door handle and opened the door cautiously. A bell over the door jingled. We waited a few minutes and when we didn't hearing anything, went inside.

The place smelled of herbs. The pungent scent of sandalwood and patchouli wafted over me. The shop must have been cute in its time. The wall was lined with rows of amber-colored bottles filled with essential oils and books.

Large bins of potpourri, a metal washtub filled with milled soaps, and other eccentricities decorated the place.

"Can't remember what she asked for," Kellimore said as he stared at the oils.

I pulled a tote off the wall and tossed it to him. "Then take what you can carry," I said, guessing the doctor knew very well the medicinal qualities of the oils.

"Hey," Will called, "I found some candy. Looks like it's still good."

Buddie grabbed another tote and crossed the room to help Will bag up the find. I drifted over to the tea display. In Georgetown, there was a small tea shop just a few blocks from my apartment. I used to spend Saturday morning there eating lemon scones, sipping tea, and catching up with work on my laptop. It was a Saturday morning ritual that belonged to a life that seemed so distant to me now. I eyed the shelves and pulled down a bag of my favorite brand, The Dreaming Wood, but movement outside got my attention. I set the bag on the counter and went to the window. In the yard across the street, I spotted one of the undead.

"I'll be back in a minute," I called then headed outside.

I pushed the door open as quietly as I could, not wanting the undead man to see me. He was standing under a tree in the yard of a small white house. His plaid shirt was in tatters, his emaciated body no longer able to hold up the jeans that hung loose around his waist. Wisps of shaggy dark hair clung to his head. Large, red fissures marred his skin making his face a mottled mess. He stood slack-jawed, most of the flesh around his mouth decayed. The flesh on his arm had wilted away, leaving only pulpy-looking flesh, sinew, and bone.

I moved slowly off the porch and glanced around me. I didn't see anyone else. Nothing was moving, neither alive nor undead. There was only the single, decayed creature.

Taking a deep breath, I stepped toward him. Using just my mind, I called to him *"You. Do you hear me?"*

The undead man didn't move.

I tried again. *"Here. I'm here. Do you see me?"*

Again, there was nothing. Frustrated, I pulled my sword and crossed this street.

"Hey, buddy, wake up," I shouted with my mind. This time, undead man turned and lumbered toward me. *"Stop,"* I told him, using my mind. Hissing, he still came toward me. "Stop," I said again, this time out loud, but still he didn't relent. Mindlessly, he stumbled toward me.

Sighing, I quickly stabbed him through the head. He hung there for a moment. Pulling my blade, I shook him off, his head sliding from the steel before he crumpled on the ground.

Behind me, the door opened and shut.

"Any more?" Will called.

"Not that I saw."

Kellimore crossed the street, joining me, then squatted to look over the man. "Mister Greene," he said. "That's his house. We went through it though. Must have overlooked him."

"Look," Buddie said, motioning to a shed in the back. A tree branch had fallen on the corner of the shed, crushing the wall. "You check in there?"

Kellimore shook his head then looked down at the man. "Nasty piece of work. He yelled at my sister for crying too loud when she wrecked her bike on his sidewalk...just there," he said, pointing. "Her knee was bleeding like hell. He actually screamed at her for bawling. I carried her and that bike all the way home. I was covered in blood by the time we got there," he said, then his voice faded.

"Your sister?" I asked gently.

Kellimore shook his head, and I saw him quickly dash a tear from his eye. "One of the first to go. I had to..."

I put my hand on his shoulder.

"Eh," Kellimore said, stepping away, "serves you right," he told Mister Greene then waved to us. "Come on. We'll go around the lake then head back."

Buddie, Will, and I followed behind. I looked back at Mister Greene. Maybe I was losing my damned mind. Maybe the tea that Grandma had given me had just confused my senses. I could just be imaging everything, the stress of it all getting to me. I didn't know what to think. Had he heard me or had he seen me? He hadn't responded and he hadn't stopped. I wasn't sure what to think. Either way, I didn't have my answer yet.

LAYLA

The sun was high in the sky when we finished canvasing the streets surrounding half the lake. There were no further signs of the undead anywhere.

"Main Street is split into two halves," Kellimore told us when we intersected the street once more on the opposite side of the lake. "This is south Main Street," he explained as he led us down the main thoroughfare. The street was lined in autumnal decorations just as it had been on the other side of the lake. Small boutiques, shops, and restaurants lined the way.

"Look there," Buddie said, motioning to what looked like an old movie theater.

"That's the old Granville Theater."

"Look at the door," Buddie said.

What Kellimore had missed was that not only was the door slightly ajar, someone had broken a small hole in the glass door to get to the handle. Shards of glass glimmered on the ground.

"What the hell," Kellimore exclaimed then stomped toward the theater.

Buddie grabbed his arm, pulling him back. "Easy," he said. His eyes drifted across the building. "How many other entrances?"

Kellimore shook his head. "Just one, in the back. It's a single screen theater. They kept the place open to show old movies. It's dark inside, theater floor dug into a slope in the ground, real old style."

"No windows," Will observed. "Keeps the light out."

"Dark. Shuttered," Buddie added.

My skin rose in goosebumps. Could Rumor's people have followed us here? Could they be watching this place? The pattern was the same. Just like in Hamletville, first we saw an influx of zombies. Then the vampires came, once everyone was rattled enough to believe whatever story they wanted to sell.

"You think someone's in there?" Kellimore asked. "Then we need to go inside, check it out. You're all armed. Let's go."

I gazed up at the sun. It was midafternoon. There was still several hours of daylight left. Surely, we were being paranoid, but it didn't pay to take chances.

"Where does the back door lead?" Buddie asked.

"There is a parking lot in the back."

"Layla?" Buddie asked.

I exhaled deeply and tried to concentrate. My feelings were distracted. *See*, my grandmother had said. I closed my eyes. I felt...something. I opened my eyes and nodded. "Let's open the doors, let the sun in...just in case."

"Why?" Kellimore asked, looking puzzled.

"I like to see what's around the next corner."

Shrugging, Kellimore crossed the street with us. We entered the building slowly, the broken glass crunching underfoot. Inside, the theater had the smell of old carpet and stale popcorn. The carpet was deep red. Posters of black and white movies adorned the place. There was a concession stand in the center of the space. Behind it was an open foyer and double theater doors. The doors were shut.

Working quietly, we opened the blinds and propped the doors open. Sunlight bathed the place. If my guess was right, the sun would shine into the movie theater once the doors were open. If there was anyone inside, they wouldn't be able to hide very well.

"Don't rush in," I told Kellimore as I stood with my hand on the theater door.

Buddie knocked an arrow and Will gripped his baseball bat tighter.

"You all look like you're expecting...company," Kellimore observed.

"Let's just say we've learned to be careful," I replied then tugged on the theater door. To my surprise, it opened easily. I pulled the door back and pushed it to the side then opened the second door.

I pulled my shashka from its scabbard.

Long slants of light shone into the theater, illuminating much of the space, but the corners were still shrouded in darkness.

Casting a glance back at the concession stand, I found what I was looking for. Sitting along the counter were at least a dozen flashlights. In an old-style theater, they'd still had ushers.

I grabbed the flashlights and handed one to everyone. Moving carefully, we went inside.

The theater walls were covered in thick, red velvet draping. Gold-colored sconces caught flecks of light shining in from outside. I flashed my light all around the corners of the theater and bent my ear to listen. I couldn't hear anything. Buddie motioned for us to spread out and we slowly worked our way into the theater. The place had a rank, musty smell. The massive screen hung like a blank canvas. There was a large crystal chandelier overhead. The cut glass tinkled as a soft breeze pushed through the place. My heart was beating hard as I scanned all around. While I didn't see anything, all of my senses were on edge. I watched as the others moved through the theater, their flashlights panning between rows and in corners. Kellimore moved more boldly than the rest of us, thinking he was hunting squatters, or at worst, zombies. I wanted to tell him there was worse in the world out there.

Our search didn't turn up anyone, but when I reached the front of the theater, I shined my flashlight down the front row and discovered a bag and some papers lying on the floor. Moving slowly, I went to investigate. The papers scattered on the floor revealed a map of the town. I grabbed the backpack and opened it. Inside, I found several changes of clothes, guns, and empty plastic water bottles.

I was about to call out to Buddie when I spotted another slip of paper lying on the ground. I bent to pick it up. It took me a minute to register that the notes thereon had been written in Russian.

"Buddie," I called, but just as he turned to look, a gust of wind slammed into the room, and the theater doors clapped shut, drowning us in darkness.

"Wind," Kellimore called as he started back up the aisle toward the door.

"Wait," I called to him. Then, I heard it.

Just as I had at the HarpWind, I began to hear muffled voices ringing inside my head. I couldn't make out the words, the voices sounding as if I was hearing them from underwater. The sound seemed to come from every corner of the room. I panned my flashlight all around. The beam of light cast long shadows where Buddie, Will, and Kellimore stood. But then, as the others flashed around, I saw them. Other shadows, other figures, were moving among the beams of light, casting faint shadows on the wall.

"Dammit, it's locked," Kellimore called. "Layla, you're close to the back exit, give the door a try."

I breathed in slowly, exhaling quietly as I scanned all around. Where were they?

I set the bag down, clicked off my flashlight, and held my shashka with two hands as I backed toward the door. The battery-powered exit light shimmered green. The door wasn't more than thirty feet from me.

"Layla," Buddie called, flashing his light around. "We're in trouble."

My skin rose in gooseflesh as I backed toward the door. My nerves were set on edge as I felt, but couldn't see, someone near me. I swished my blade in front of me. I felt just the slightest pressure on the tip of the blade, almost as if I had cut through fabric. Then I caught the subtlest of smells: a strange, musty, rotted scent assailed my nose. Moving quickly, I spun my blade in a circle all around me and heard a hiss in the darkness in reply.

Will was stone silent as he shone his light all around the room. In the glare of the flashlight, for just a moment, I caught the reflection of a moon-white face.

"You see that?" Kellimore called. "There's someone in here."

"Sh," Buddie whispered.

Reaching out with my free hand, I slid it along the wall behind me, feeling for the doorframe. I gasped when I felt cloth brush against my hand.

"Move, or I'll have your head," I whispered into the darkness and shifted my blade in front of me.

A female voice giggled, and this time, I heard it clearly. Whoever it was moved away.

"Who's in here?" Kellimore called. "Show yourself."

Dammit, he was going to get himself killed. I grabbed for the handle, said a silent prayer that the door was unlocked, and pushed the lever. The door was sticky, but a moment later, it opened, bathing the room in air and light.

From somewhere above, I heard the giggle once more and saw a shadow move in the small balcony hanging above the seats. I hadn't noticed it before. The men rushed toward me and out the door.

I looked back down the aisle. The backpack and papers were gone. The paper written in Russian, however, was still clenched in my hand. I stared at it. On it, someone had been keeping a list. It named towns in Maryland, West Virginia, and Pennsylvania. In addition to the place names, there were number tallies and other notes. The final entry read "Claddagh-Basel College, 76 survivors, clean blood. Children of Koschei minimal."

I turned and joined the men outside. The door banged closed behind me.

"What the hell was that?" Kellimore asked. He looked pale and shaken.

"Trouble," Buddie answered.

I stared back at the note. My grandmother had told me many folktales about Koschei, a trickster in the old stories. While most of the tales involved him tricking maidens out of their virginity, there was one fact about Koschei that always kept me awake at night long after Grandma had gone to sleep. Koschei was a walking skeleton, a living dead man.

LAYLA
14

As we headed back to the college, one thought echoed through my mind. I needed to get to Jaime, to my people. I needed to make sure they were safe. I needed to get everyone together. These might not have been Rumor's vampires, but they were vampires. And they were hunting. Once my people were safe, I'd have to find a way to warn the college survivors. That was easier said than done. Something told me that Doctor Gustav was not a believer. But Tristan seemed to be a different story. The only other problem we had now was Kellimore.

"I need to come back with some armed men. We need to turn that place inside out. Someone is holed up in there. Someone...bad," Kellimore was saying, his face full of fury.

"Hold tight, brother," Will said then. "Let's get back first then decide what to do. But whatever we're going to do, we need to do it soon," he added, casting an eye to the sky.

"Get all the Hamletville people back into the library and tell them to stay put until I give an all clear," I told Buddie who nodded. "Didn't Cricket say there is a chapel in the college? Do you know where that is?" I asked, turning to Kellimore.

"Yeah, on the first floor there is a small place," he replied, looking perplexed.

"You and Kellimore go there and get stocked up on…" I said then paused, looking at Will.

He nodded to me. "I understand."

"I need to find Tristan…and Vella. Do you have a way to get all your people together for a meeting?" I asked Kellimore.

He nodded. "We meet up in the Student Union."

"Get the supplies then get your people together in the Student Union," I told Kellimore.

I kept one eye on the sun as we moved. It was going to be close. Dusk was no more than an hour away. When we arrived, Joe was sleeping in a lawn chair by the gate. The other guard was missing.

"We're back," Kellimore said, waking Joe.

The man rose slowly and opened the gate.

"You see any sign of trouble here?" Kellimore asked.

"No, why? You see something?" Joe asked.

"Joe, we thought we saw someone in town. Can you get a couple more men on the gate?" I said then, interrupting what would likely be a long answer.

He nodded. "Frank will be back in a minute. Needed to find a tree to, well, you know. I'll have him bring a couple more guys down. Something spook you?" he asked me, looking worried.

I nodded.

"Kell?" he said then, turning to Kellimore.

Kellimore nodded. "We'll call a meeting. Keep your eyes open."

"I'll meet you in the library," I said to Buddie then turned and headed down the walkway that led to the doctor's lab.

"Why are we going to the chapel again?" Kellimore was asking Will as they moved away.

Knowing Will, I was sure he could come up with a good reply. I hated to scare these people. Like us, they had found a sanctuary. But all that seemed like it was about to come unglued. Unless we were ready, the Claddagh-Basel survivors could fall prey just like we did. I wouldn't let it happen again.

As I rounded the side of the building, I eyed the fence line. Behind the back wall was a thick woods. It could provide good cover in a pinch. The stone fence was sturdy and would keep out any undead, but it wouldn't withstand vampires. As my eyes scanned down the fence line, I was surprised to see a tuft of russet-orange fur: a fox. The creature sat very still, watching me.

I stopped in my tracks, suppressing a gasp.

The fox rose and took a couple of steps toward me.

"You bitch," I swore then pulled my sword and started crossing the lawn toward the fox.

The fox turned and dodged toward the fence, escaping through a very small gap between the rocks.

I stopped mid-step. Surely, not every fox was a shapeshifter. But still. "I know what you did," I called. "And I won't forget."

I was met with silence.

Maybe I was going crazy. I was shouting at wild animals. My poor mind could barely keep track of all the ways the world was turning. I felt like my brain was tumbling in a dryer. Sighing, I headed back toward the college, entering the corridor where the doctor's lab was housed. The hallway was cool and quiet.

The light was on inside the lab. I opened the door to find the lab was empty. The doctor's beakers still boiled, blue fire blazing underneath, but no one was there. Someone had, however, rolled a massive wooden case into the room. It was locked up. I walked between the tables, looking at the doctor's notes. She was looking at everything, food, preservatives, cosmetics, water samples. She also had page after page of notes on genetics. From her notes, however, what she seemed particularly interested in at the moment was the flu vaccine and genetically modified food. In another notebook, she was tracking the effectiveness of various vaccine concoctions. I cast a glance at the rats. Was she testing vaccines on them? But they didn't look sick. At the bottom of her notes, however, she'd written in big letters: "Need more test subjects! Ready for trails!"

Just then, I heard a clatter in one of the closed contamination rooms.

"Hello?" I called.

No answer.

I paused and listened. It was so silent in this space, but still, I could feel someone nearby.

"Hello?" I called, this time using my mind.

I was met by a strange sounding *"humph"* in my head. The sound seemed to come from behind one of the closed doors. I crossed the room and set my hand on one of the doorknobs. Locked. Gently, I tapped on the door. From the other side, I heard the dulled rattle of chains.

"Layla?" someone called from behind.

Startled, I jumped and turned to find Jaime behind me. He was holding a small case in his hands.

"Sorry, I didn't mean to scare you."

"Just startled me," I replied. "What's in there?"

Jaime closed the door to the lab behind him. "Don't freak out," he said quietly. "She has one of the undead chained up in there."

"What the hell? Why?"

"She needed a specimen. In fact, you came just in time to help me. She sent me to get a sample."

"A sample of what?"

"Blood. Well, as close to blood as they have."

Jaime crossed the room and pulled a key from his pocket. He unlocked the door with a click. "Step back a minute," he said.

I did as he asked but pulled my shashka all the same.

Inside the small room, which looked like it had once been a closet, was one of the decaying undead. The man, who must have been small in stature when alive, was chained by the neck and arms to a pole. His clothing was in tatters, and I could see that someone had taken a very big bite out of his neck, exposing him down to the shoulder. The terrible smell of decay wafted off him. He bit and snapped, bloody saliva dripping down his chin.

"Jaime," I said warningly. But I didn't know what to say. I understood why, but that didn't mean it felt right.

"It startled me too, at first. But she's really discovering some things, maybe even on the way to finding a cure. But without testing on him, we'll never know."

I stared at the man. *"Hello?"*

There was no reply, only biting and snapping. But I felt this strange sense in the air. It was the same feeling you get when you are in the middle of a conversation with someone and they won't answer you, their words hanging unspoken.

Jaime grabbed a chain on the floor. "Sorry, fella," he said then gave it a tug, pulling the undead man tight against the pole. Once the man was firmly locked down, unable to reach out for a grab or bite, Jaime locked the chain then opened the small case he was carrying. "They don't have blood, per se," he told me, "but she showed me their fluids under the slides. There is something animating them. Kiki and Doctor Gustav have been up in the attic trying to set up some equipment to run on solar power. That girl sure has a mechanical mind.

"Just imagine if we can find the cause," he said as he approached the undead man. "Keep your blade on him in case he yanks his arms off just trying to get to me." Jaime knelt, pulled on a pair of medical gloves, and then took out a syringe, uncapping it with his teeth. He grabbed the undead man's leg, which was exposed from a cut in his pants, then stabbed the creature with the needle.

I stared at the undead man who tried to look down as he snapped at Jaime. Tristan was right. This was weird science. Jaime filled three syringes with a strange yellowish-red liquid, setting each one in the case, before he finally rose.

"Done." He peeled of the gloves and motioned for me to go back into the lab. Unlocking the chains, the undead man lunged at Jaime, but the chain snapped him back in time. Jaime exited the room behind me, closing and locking the door behind him.

"Something about this seems wrong," I told Jaime.

He shrugged. "Took me a minute too, but how many have we killed? At least she has purpose," he said then looked at me. "What's wrong, Layla? Sorry, I was so focused when I came in that I missed it. What's the matter?"

"We have a problem," I said then told Jaime what we had come across at the theater.

"Vampires from the HarpWind?"

"I don't think so. We killed most of them, and the others wouldn't have had time to make it to safety before the sun rose. These vampires seem like they're just hunting. Look," I said, showing him the paper.

"What if these creatures have been living among us everywhere? Is it possible there are...a lot of them?" Jaime asked.

"We didn't see any in Hamletville."

"If you were a vampire, would you live in Hamletville?"

I had to chuckle. Considering I didn't even want to live there, I guessed not. But I didn't want to say so. For all his worldliness, Jaime was a hometown boy. "No."

"How are we going to tell them?"

"We're not. We'll tell Tristan. He can tell them."

"And how do you know he'll believe you."

"I just know."

"Why?"

What could I say? There was something about Tristan that wasn't quite…I didn't know what. But I suspected he heard me call to that undead man outside the school that morning. And then there was that glow to him. I had seen a glow like that before…on Peryn. "Because…because he isn't human either."

CRICKET

"What in the world is going on?" I asked as Vella, Darius, Ariel, Chase, and I made our way down the hall toward the Student Union.

Vella shook her head, but she seemed preoccupied as she played with her cards. I hated it when she did that. It always gave me the feeling something bad was about to happen, but more often than not those cards got us out of a jam, so I tried to stay patient until Vella decided what she needed to say.

"Kellimore's been rounding everyone up. He said they saw someone in town earlier today," Chase replied.

"Of course he did," Ariel said then rolled her eyes.

"He'll have us all hunting a mannequin again," Darius said with a laugh.

"True that, but I don't blame him for getting worked up about that mannequin. Creepy ass things. Who leaves a mannequin sitting in front of a window?" Chase replied.

"A dressmaker," Vella answered absently.

"Ain't that the truth," Chase replied.

I had to chuckle. Kellimore had made some mistakes along the way, but most of the time his instincts were good. He loved his town the way I had loved the carnival. It was like he took keeping the place safe personal. Sometimes he acted like a jerk, but I admired his dedication.

"Someone said Kellimore went out with Layla and a couple of her guys," Chase said.

Now I was worried. "For real? They saw someone too?"

Chase nodded.

"Hey, where's Tristan?" Ariel asked.

"In the woods," Vella answered, then stopped, making all of us stop with her.

"What is it?" Chase asked.

Vella looked up at us, a haunted expression on her face. "There is great danger here." She held out a card for all of us to see. On it was a skeleton figure in armor riding on a horse. "Death."

"Wait, is someone going to die?" Ariel whispered, asking the question we were all thinking.

I felt like someone had poured ice water over my head.

Vella shook her head. "Not quite. He is the personification of death, but in our world, death walks. We must be cautious."

We were about to head into the Student Union when Elle rushed up behind me. "Cricket," she said, out of breath. "There are two people at the gate. They want to come in. Joe sent me for someone, and I can't find Doctor Gustav or Tristan anywhere. Kellimore's got everyone spooked. They don't know if they should let them in or not."

I looked at Vella.

"All right, I'll go check 'em out," I said. "Can you stay put, try to keep a lid on Kellimore?" I asked Elle.

She nodded.

"But you, you're coming with me," I told Vella.

She slipped her cards back into her bag then nodded.

"I'll come too. I'm still carrying," he said, patting his gun.

"I don't like this," Vella told Darius and Ariel. "Go find some place quiet and stay hidden."

"Faculty lounge," Darius said. "We'll be there." He took Ariel's hand and they turned and headed the opposite direction of the Student Union.

"You suppose it will be death on a horse?" I asked Vella as we turned and headed outside.

"I don't know what it will be," Vella replied.

Her answer made me nervous.

Outside, the sun had just dipped below the horizon. The last of the sunset had painted the sky with pale hues of orange and purple. There was a mist creeping up from the lake. It was always like that, the mist settling in at night and not rising again until noon. There were days when I never thought we'd see the sun. The spring air was cool. I pulled my flannel shirt closed, buttoning it.

"Cold, Cricket?" Chase asked. "You can take my coat."

"I'll be all right, but thanks," I told him.

Vella's dark eyes studied the figures at the gate as we approached. I didn't like the look on her face. And the air itself felt real tingly. I hadn't felt anything like that since that day at Fairway Fun when Tristan saved my life.

Chase pulled his gun. I did the same, and kept my hand on my wrench to boot. We approached the gate real slow. I could see that Joe, Frank, and Andy were holding guns on the two people on the other side.

"We got visitors, Joe?" I called, trying to sound chipper.

"Yep," he called back, a sullen tone in his voice.

In the dimming twilight, I could just make out the faces of the two strangers. Both wore black coats with hoods that shadowed their faces. The girl looked to be about my age. She had long brown hair that curled down her chest. She was strikingly beautiful, but very pale. She had a backpack strung across her back. There was a man with her, a hulking creature with dark hair and ice-blue eyes.

"Evenin'" I said.

"Hello," the girl replied. "We're looking for sanctuary. We've been on the road awhile. We thought we saw some people in town today. I think we might have frightened them. Really sorry about that. We were staying at the old theater downtown. We were hoping we could come in? We ran out of food two days back, and we're both really starving."

"What's your name?" Vella asked her.

The girl turned her head with an odd twitch and looked Vella over. It was then that I realized that her eyes were the same icy blue as the man's. "Sarah, and this is Giles."

"Where y'all from?" I asked.

Giles looked at me, and I could tell by the expression on his face that he was choking in frustration. I didn't care if he didn't like my questions. All things considered, these two had set my nerves on edge. That, coupled with Vella's cards, left me feeling none too friendly. Not to mention I was still in a bad mood over my fight with Tristan.

"We've been travelling, but I'm from Boston," the girl answered.

"What about you?" I asked Giles.

"The same," he replied. He had an odd accent. I'd been through Boston a few times with the carnival. That didn't sound like a Massachusetts accent to me.

"What's in the bag?" I asked.

Sarah shifted nervously. "Just some supplies."

"You want in, hand it through the gate."

Giles gave her a sharp look, but she handed the backpack through the bars all the same.

"I don't want you to get the wrong idea," Sarah said as Chase went to retrieve the backpack. "Whenever we find a gun, we grab it. We don't have hardly any ammo, but we've run across some bad people. Lots of people getting killed out here."

She didn't have to tell me. I'd never forget seeing Gemma shot in the back and the cries of those poor little girls as they were gunned down.

Chase emptied the bag onto the ground. Inside were several changes of clothes, guns, and empty water bottles. "No food?" he asked.

Sarah shook her head. "We ran out."

I looked at Giles who was looking at Joe and the others, his eyes moving from one person to the next. When his eyes landed on Vella, he looked away.

I turned my back, facing away from them, then whispered to Vella. "Well?"

"Don't let them in," she said.

"Agreed," I replied.

I turned back. "We don't have much by way of supplies either, but we'll pack your bag for you. Joe, mind heading up to the pantry? Stock up their bag and bring it back, please."

"You...you aren't going to invite us in?" Sarah asked. She wore an expression like she was trying to smolder rage.

"No," Vella said then. "You are *not* invited inside," she said sternly.

"What's going on here?" a voice called from behind me.

I turned to see Doctor Gustav coming down the walkway toward us.

"Just some folks passin' through," I told her.

Doctor Gustav adjusted her glasses and looked at the pair.

"We asked to come in," Sarah told the doctor. "We're exhausted. My brother and I have been travelling for days."

"Either of you infected?" Doctor Gustav asked.

"No," Sarah answered. "Just hungry," she added with a smile.

"I was about to have Joe grab them some supplies so they can keep movin'," I said when Doctor Gustav reached out and unlocked the gate.

"No need for that," the doctor said then motioned for them to enter. "Come inside. Get some rest," she said.

Sarah smiled nicely at the doctor. "Thank you," she said. "Thank you so much." She then turned to me. "Don't blame you. No hard feelings."

"We'll be keeping these," Chase said as he closed up the backpack.

"I understand," Sarah answered. "We don't need them anyway."

"Come along," the doctor said then. "It's nearly dinner time."

"Great," Sarah said then, winking at Vella, she and Giles followed the doctor back toward the building.

"They didn't seem so bad," Joe said then. "The girl, whew, those were some eyes."

I looked at Vella.

"We need to find Tristan. Now," she said, then took me by the arm and pulled me in the direction of the big tree.

"Something isn't right here," Chase said as he followed along behind us.

"That's an understatement," Vella said.

I sighed heavily. I just hated this. "What is it, Vella? What's going on?"

"We need Tristan."

"Why?"

"Because if we have any hope of surviving, we'll need his help."

"Why? Who were they?"

"Strigoi," Vella answered.

"What's a strigoi?" I asked as we hustled across the green in the fog toward the old oak.

Vella stopped and turned to face us both. "Vampire."

LAYLA

Jaime and I exited the side of the building and headed around the back of the college in the direction of the Student Union.

"What are you going to say?" Jaime asked.

"I don't know," I replied, shaking my head.

Jaime reached out and took my hand. "Layla."

I stopped and looked at him. I'd barely had a moment to process what had shifted between Jaime and me. Our night together had been unexpected but wonderful. But ever since we left Hamletville, we'd done nothing but run. I was beginning to wonder if I could ever go back to being just a person again.

Jaime leaned in and kissed me, his hand sliding up the nape of my neck. "I love you so much," he whispered.

"I love you too."

"We need to survive this. The doctor may be able to end this so we can have a chance at a normal life."

Jaime's words echoed my thoughts. I didn't have the heart to tell him that I feared it wasn't possible anymore. Whatever kind of living there was to be done from now on, it didn't look anything like it had before. But I loved him, and I wanted him to have hope. "Then we'll do whatever we can to help her."

Jaime kissed my forehead and we walked through the mist toward the other end of the building. The sun had set. The last hues of purple barely kissed the horizon. I'd have to convince everyone fast.

In the dimming light, however, I saw four figures walking across the lawn toward us. I pulled my blade. Cricket, Vella, Tristan, and Chase emerged from the mist and came into view.

"Layla? That you?" There was no mistaking Cricket's accent.

"Yes, I was looking for Tristan."

As Tristan stepped forward, I again saw that strange glow emanating from him. It was like someone was shining a light on him, a strange glimmer of gold and green surrounding just him. He looked worried, as did the rest of the group. Something told me they already knew. Vella. Vella's face told the tale.

"You were looking for me?" Tristan asked.

"We saw trouble in town. I thought you might have some...perspective on how to best warn the people here."

"They're already here," Vella said then.

"What?"

"The doctor invited them in. They're inside."

"I still think y'all have lost it. I mean, that's just unbelievable," Cricket said then.

"No more unbelievable than zombies," Jaime told her.

Cricket paused, surprised by his interruption.

"This is not your first encounter with the nightwalkers?" Tristan asked.

"No, nor other kinds of beings," I replied, looking pointedly at him. "Which is why I was looking for you. Do you know Peryn?"

Cricket frowned.

Tristan inclined his head to me.

"Can you help me?"

"The nightwalkers are our ancient enemy. There is a blood feud between us. I will do everything I can to stop them, to protect the ones I love," Tristan said.

"Blood feud between you and who? The vampires?" Cricket asked, sounding frustrated. "Tristan, what in the world are you saying?"

Tristan turned to her, gently stroked her cheek, and then said, "I told you I would make it right. Tonight," he told her then turned back to me. "We'd better hurry before they charm them all."

"Or eat them," Jaime said under his breath.

"Man, come on," Chase said, looking at Jaime.

"No joke," Jaime replied, turning serious. "Some of their kind took my brother."

Chase looked like he was still trying to accept what he was hearing. "Sorry."

Jaime nodded.

"How many?" I asked, turning to Vella.

"Only two."

"Why did the doctor let them in?" I asked, perplexed.

Cricket shook her head. "That got me too. She's usually more careful."

I saw Jaime shift a bit, like he had an idea, but he didn't say anything.

"What do we do?" Vella asked.

"I have an idea," I replied, then looked at Tristan. "Got my back?"

He nodded.

"We all do," Cricket said, twirling her pipe wrench.

17

LAYLA

The scene was like an echo of the events that took place in the gymnasium in Hamletville. Once again, the vampires were at the front of the room speaking. Once again, the innocent people listened, completely oblivious to what was happening. This time, however, my people were safe. Only Will was in the room, leaning against the back wall, a shoebox stuffed under his arm. Buddie had kept the other survivors out of harm's way. With a little luck, they'd never have to see this sight again.

Tristan pulled up the hood on his jacket, covering his face. Taking Cricket's hand, they moved toward the edge of the room near the front. I noticed then that Cricket looked perturbed. For some reason, I didn't think she knew what, exactly, the man she loved actually was. And it looked like, for the first time, she was beginning to realize he wasn't what he appeared. That, coupled with the sudden appearance of vampires, would surely have anyone on edge.

Chase stood at the back, gun drawn.

The vampires were still talking, telling everyone what they had seen on the road, when we entered. But under that talk, I heard their muffled, telepathic speech. They were having a second conversation. And as of yet, it seemed as if they hadn't noticed us.

Will handed me the box. I lifted the lid to find two full water bottles inside.

"Sure it's the right thing? Otherwise, we're in for a... show," I whispered.

"Positive," Will replied.

I handed a bottle to Jaime and gave the other to Will. "On him. On my word," I whispered.

They nodded and we moved toward the front of the crowd. We worked slowly, pushing through the others, until we were at the front. Kellimore was leaning against a table watching the newcomers with a frustrated expression on his face. Opposite him, Elle was staring at Sarah. She was frowning.

"It was just horrible," the female vampire was saying as her crystal eyes scanned the room. She was sitting in a chair, the male standing a few feet away from her. "They were just torturing that poor family. We barely got away..."

Lies. "You know, I'm sick of vampires," I said then motioned to Will and Jaime.

Jaime, remembering how fast the vampires could shift, moved fast, dashing holy water over Giles. Will was right behind him. The men splashed the vampire, who must have heard my words, because he had turned to face me a split second before we attacked. When the water blasted him, however, he shrieked and clutched his face.

"What the hell," Kellimore shouted, standing.

"Someone stop them! They threw acid on him," one of the college residents yelled.

Kellimore moved forward.

"No," Tristan shouted, freezing Kellimore's steps.

The male vampire crumpled to the ground, writhing, as black smoke engulfed him.

The college people screamed and fled toward the back of the room.

The female vampire jumped to her feet, but not before I could move in and get a blade against her throat. She froze, but her eyes darted toward Tristan. "You," she hissed. "You tired creature. Where's your ward?"

"Shut up," I told her.

"Stop," I heard Doctor Gustav yell from the back of the room. "Stop this instant."

I ignored her.

"And what will you do if I don't, human?" the vampire replied.

"Well, you're not the first vampire I've killed this week," I hissed back at her. "But I have something special in mind for you," I replied. Lunging forward, I jabbed one of Jaime's undead blood-filled needles into the woman's chest and emptied its contents under her skin. I was hedging a bet, but if I was right, maybe we could finally get some answers. Otherwise, a battle was about to be underway.

The vampire looked at me aghast. "What have you done?" she whispered.

"Welcome back," I replied.

The woman fell to the floor and started convulsing.

"What is happening here?" Doctor Gustav demanded as she pushed to the front of the room. I saw her eyes go wide as she stared at what was left of the male vampire. "What... what happened to him? What did you throw on him?" she asked Jaime.

"Holy water," Jaime replied.

"Holy water?"

"They're vampires," Jaime told her.

The doctor adjusted her glasses and looked at the woman convulsing on the floor.

After a few moments, the vampire's body went still.

Jaime bent down and felt her wrist. He nodded to me.

"What was in the syringe?" Tristan asked.

I looked around. Most of the room had cleared out. Kellimore and Elle watched on in disbelief.

"The blood, per se, of a zombie. Their bite has an odd effect on vampires. It returns them to a mortal life," I replied.

"Well this just gets more and more interesting," Cricket said. She was visibly upset.

Just then, the female vampire took a deep, shuddering breath and sat straight up, gasping for air. She looked up at me. Her eyes were dark brown, her cheeks red. She lifted her hands and looked at them, then set her hand on her heart. She looked shocked when she felt it beating.

"I am still a dead woman," she said, looking at me. "And so are you."

"How many of you are there?"

"I'm one of you again. For the moment."

"You know what I mean."

She started to breathe heavily. "Not many," she replied. "Not anymore. We used to have many hives. Now we're just a few scattered groups."

"I found your list," I said, showing her the list of towns, the numbers of survivors. "What are you doing? Stalking us?"

She shrugged, but her labored breathing intensified. "Our queen sent us on a mission. We're starving, and we need your blood. There is no way you can escape us. We can smell you from a hundred miles away."

"Your queen? Do you mean Rumor?"

The woman coughed heavily but stared at me aghast. "How…how did you know?"

"Because we killed her two days back, and burned your hotel."

"No," she whispered aghast.

"How did you find us?"

"We hadn't even meant to come here," she said, coughing hard. "We got turned around in the fog. But something led us here."

"Something? What?"

"A…" she said, but then paused to cough hard. Blood sputtered from her mouth. "A fox."

"A fox?" Cricket said with a half-laugh, half-grunt.

The vampire looked at me. "I've been alive since 1881. There is no day without night. As long as you live, we can live too. And to that end, we will never stop hunting you," she said then started wheezing.

I knelt down so I could look her in the eyes. "Maybe not, but I can kill you…all of you."

"You can try," she said, then surprising me, she grabbed both my arms. "But you will fail." She then took a deep, pained breath and stiffened. As she held onto my arms, a change came over her. Her body, like it was drying up from the inside, seemed to petrify before my very eyes. Her eyes rolled back into her head, and her long, dark-colored locks faded to gray, then to white. Her flesh shriveled until it was withered like a mummy. Her eyes disappeared inside her head, skin around her face drying and decaying. Moments later, I sat face-to-face with a rotted corpse. Doctor Madala was right. The vampires do return to life with all their diseases intact. But what the doctor didn't seem to know was that they also returned intact at the same age they truly were. And, if that were true, despite the vampire's dark words, they could be killed.

"I think I'm going to throw up," I heard Cricket whisper.

I shook the vampire's hand off my arms and stood, letting her body slump over sideways.

Doctor Gustav stepped forward and leaned over the body. She lifted the arm, investigated it, and then set it back down. "I guess I shouldn't have let them in," she said then rose and looked at Jaime. "We'll get a gurney then take the bodies back to my lab and get some samples," she told him then turned to me. "Seems you're rather handy to have around."

"Just unlucky. A group of vampires lured us from our home. That's how we ended up here."

"But you've found a way to fight them," Tristan said.

I nodded.

"Very well," the doctor said then turned to Kellimore and Elle. "Go check on everyone. Tell them everything is safe now, but tell them what we've seen. Tell them the truth."

"And what in the hell is the truth?" Kellimore asked as he gazed at the bodies of the two dead vampires lying on the ground.

"That there are two breeds of undead among us. The college is now on lockdown at night. Three guards on the gate, and they must be armed with," she said then looked at me, "holy water. Dusk curfew. If anyone has any questions, they can talk to Layla. Tristan, I'll leave the rest to you," the doctor said then began moving away. "Jaime? Can you assist me?"

He looked at me.

"Go. I'm going to go upstairs and check on the others."

Jaime nodded then followed the doctor out the door.

Tristan and Cricket were speaking in low tones. Taking her by the hand, Tristan led Cricket out of the room. I heard the door leading outside clap shut.

"Someone said Kiki was still working in the attic," Will said, his voice sounding anxious.

"Please check on her."

Will nodded then left, leaving only Vella and me standing in the room.

"Strigoi," she said then, looking down at the bodies.

"Cricket doesn't know about Tristan, does she?"

Vella shook her head.

"You can see the other side too. The undead, have you ever…heard them?"

Vella shook her head. "Have you?"

"I don't know."

"Then you must see."

My grandmother's words. "I'm trying."

Vella smiled at me. "Try harder."

LAYLA

"There were vampires? Here?" Tom asked aghast.

"Mommy," Susan whimpered, leaning in close to her mother. Thankfully, Kira was already asleep on one of the sofas.

"Were," I replied. "There were only two. They were hunting," I said, then told them what had happened.

"We had a hard time believing you, honey," Ethel told me. "You did them a favor to just show them. But she said there are more?"

"They were getting a tally of where the human survivors are. And guess who put her up to the task?"

"Rumor?" Tom asked.

I nodded. "It seems there's no escaping them, but now we have a better sense of their numbers. We've already wiped out their hive. It seems unlikely we'll see any more of them anytime soon, but there are others out there."

"We're safe from them?" Susan asked.

"For now. But keep that water gun close."

"Now what?" Summer asked.

"Tonight we sleep. The people here just got a very rude awakening. They will need our help, our guidance. This place is protected from the undead. We can try it here for a while. Jaime is convinced the doctor might be on to something."

"The doctor...you think it's possible?" Summer asked.

I wanted to say no. "I hope so," I said, but even as I said it I didn't believe it.

I went to the window and looked out. I could see Kellimore at the gate talking to three men. Tonight the Claddagh-Basel residents would have to face a new fear. Death had walked into their midst wearing a smile. It was strange how the most destructive powers in the world often come wrapped up in beautiful packages. I remembered my grandma's words: *beauty is deceiving*. After all, under the surface of many lived the shadow side. Until the mask slipped away, the whole word was fooled.

I don't know what time it was when Jaime finally came to bed. He wrapped his arms tight around me and fell asleep at once. I slept soundly that night. If I lay awake every night worrying about the end of the world, I'd never get any sleep. When I woke the next morning, however, Jaime was already gone.

I heard people talking in the common area of the library. Reluctantly, wanting to close my eyes for just a bit longer, I got up to see what the matter was. One thing was certain, I sure as hell wasn't interested in trouble.

I pushed open the door to see Elle, Chase, Darius, and Ariel passing out food and water.

"Good morning," I called groggily.

"Afternoon, actually," Elle said. "Everyone said to let you sleep. We figured our personal vampire slayer needed her rest."

I chuckled. "How are the others doing?" I asked Chase who handed me a pitiful looking granola bar and a can of tomato juice.

"Shaken, that's for sure. I suppose we thought we'd seen it all. Will and Kiki were downstairs this morning. They told everyone what happened to you all at that hotel. If we hadn't seen it with our own eyes, we probably would have thought you were crazy."

I nodded. "I'm sorry it had to go down like that. I hated scaring everyone."

"Well, now we know...or at least, we're trying to know," Chase replied. "Vampires," he said then shook his head.

I glanced around the room. "Where's Jaime?"

"He went back to work with the doctor," Ethel told me.

"She'll work him to death. I don't think the woman sleeps," Elle told me.

"She's driven," I said absently, still not feeling very comfortable with the idea that she was keeping a pet the others didn't know about.

"When you all are feeling up to it, why don't you come downstairs?" Ariel said. "It might make people feel better if they can talk to you."

I nodded. "Get outside, get some air," I told them. "Just stay inside the gates."

I sat then and chewed my granola bar while the others chatted with Darius, Ariel, and Elle. Chase sat down beside me.

"You're looking chewed up," he said.

"Then spit back out."

He laughed. "Everyone appreciates what you did last night. Don't know what would have happened without you."

I shrugged. "The apocalypse is really bringing out my skills," I said with a joking smile.

Chase grinned. "Darius and me are cousins. I came here with Vella, Cricket, Ariel, and Tristan," he said then looked at me. "I was wondering…Tristan…is he all right? I mean, I always had the feeling something was off, but he was good to us. Seems like you might have a sense one way or the other."

"He's all right."

Chase nodded. "Stole my girl though. Can't forgive him for that," he said with a laugh.

"Cricket?"

Chase nodded.

"Sorry."

"How 'bout her?" he said then, glancing to Frenchie.

I smirked. "What about her?"

"She got anyone?"

"Just those two little girls."

Chase nodded with a grin, clapped me on the shoulder, and then crossed the room to make a personal introduction to Frenchie. When Chase wasn't looking, she raised an eyebrow at me. I grinned at her then rose.

One thing was true about human nature. Death might throw a wrench in the works, but nothing could stop the power of love.

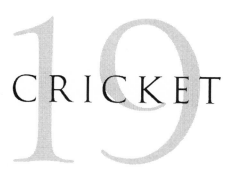

CRICKET

"Are you ready?" Tristan asked me for what seemed like the hundredth time.

"Well, I hardly know. You saying 'I'm not what I seem' doesn't tell me much considering I live in a world full of zombies and a girl in there just wiped out two vampires," I retorted sharply, motioning back to the Student Union. After Layla had killed the two vampires, I just had to get out of that place. Once again, I got the feeling my whole world was turning upside down. I should have known it was coming. From the minute Vella pulled that card, I should have known.

"Don't scream," Tristan said then. "And don't run away. I'll explain everything...after."

"After what?"

"Just watch," Tristan said then stepped back into the moonlight near the reflecting pool. The moonlight glowed real silver on him but after a minute, I realized that the glow wasn't just on him, it was coming from him. He closed his eyes and slowly a golden light swept all around him, blinding me for a minute like sunlight had shimmered into my eyes. I squeezed my eyes shut. With my eyes closed, I could tell it had gone dark again. I opened my eyes to see that Tristan was gone.

But then, a moment later, I felt something I hadn't felt in a long time: the brush of a warm nose against my hand and the feel of a sandpaper tongue. I looked down to see Puck standing there.

"Puck?" I whispered.

He sat down and whimpered, his tail wagging.

I knelt down beside him and took him by both sides of the face, scratching his ears, and looking into his eyes. "Puck?" I whispered again, looking back to where Tristan had been. I looked back into Puck's eyes, those lovely honey-brown eyes I hadn't seen in so long.

Then, I rose abruptly and took a step back. My mind swam back to the past and that moment on the carousel when Puck had died. I'd never seen his body. He'd just whimpered, and a moment later, Tristan had appeared. Tristan, who had called me by name even though we'd never met.

"Tristan?" I whispered.

Golden light swirled around Puck, blinding me once more, and when it was gone, Tristan stood where Puck had been.

My clenched hand flew to my mouth, suppressing just about every shocked exclamation that wanted to come out. I remembered my Daddy's words: *Ladies don't cuss*. Well, this lady's boyfriend had just turned into a dog—her dog—then back again.

"What the...what the Sam Hill?" I stammered.

"The devil has nothing to do with it," Tristan said as he took a step toward me.

Unconsciously, I stepped back.

"Cricket, don't be frightened. My people are here to help you. We are here to ensure mankind survives."

"Do you mean to tell me that all that time you were Puck?"

"Yes. I was sent to keep watch over you."

"Me? Why me?"

"Because you are special. Because the elders foresaw that mankind would need you during the end of days. It was my job to keep you safe. That's why I changed to save you at Fairway Fun. I'm sorry for the pain Puck's loss caused you, but I had to keep you alive."

"But you'd been running with me for more than two years before everything happened."

"Yes."

"Then you knew what was coming?"

"Yes."

"How? Why?"

"There are forces in this world that hate your kind, have been trying to destroy you for hundreds of years. They nearly succeeded during the Bubonic Plague. This time, it seems they found a way. We are not sure how, but it seems they somehow used your own devices against you. Your reign has ended, much as ours once did. Mankind has many enemies."

"Who—or maybe I should ask what—are they, the ones trying to kill us?"

"They have many names. They are the unseelie, the kitsune, the skinwalkers. They are dark earth spirits."

"And just where are they lurking? Is one of them going to jump out and try to do me in too?"

Tristan shook his head. "No. They are too clever for that. They will use the dying world itself to do their dirty work. How do you think the vampires found you? The kitsune led them here. They will bring death to your door."

"Then we are never going to be safe."

"There is hope. Layla spoke of Peryn, another of my kind. There are those of you who have the power to lead, protect. Layla is very special. I am glad you found her."

"I didn't find her. Vella did. Vella saw her. Wait, is Vella…"

"The spark of the old blood lives on in many humans. Vella has it. Layla has it. Even you have it, in a way."

"I'm no psychic."

"No, you're something better."

"And just what is that."

"A true heart."

"Now you're just diggin' too deep."

Tristan chuckled. "Cricket, I just transformed into a dog before your eyes."

"Technically, I had my eyes closed," I said then looked softly at him. "So, this is why?"

Tristan nodded. "I never meant to deceive you, to keep anything from you. I only wanted to keep you safe. But I just couldn't let us be together without you knowing the truth."

"That you aren't human."

"Well, that's not technically true. I was once human, very long ago. I was one of the first people, the fair people, they called us. But mankind changed, became brutal and bloodthirsty, and we had to leave. We went to the otherworld where time moves more slowly. And then, we became a thing of legend."

"It sounds like fairy tales."

"Interesting choice of words," Tristan said then, coming close to me, he wrapped his arms around my waist. "I'm sorry."

"For which part, lying, deceiving, letting me think Puck had died, which?"

He kissed me on the forehead then looked in my eyes. "For all of it. But I'm not sorry to have come to you as a man. And I'll remind you of something you always used to say to Puck."

"What was that?"

"You always used to tell Puck...tell me...that I was the only male you'd ever love."

"Well, I guess I didn't lie."

"I'm sorry," he whispered then pulled me into an embrace.

At long last, he'd told me the truth. I'd always wondered what the secret was. Never in my life could I have imagined it would be anything like this. But, in a way, this truth was easy to take. It was like somehow, in the back of my mind, I already knew.

"I love you," I told him.

"I love you too."

LAYLA

After downing the tomato juice, which tasted pretty sorry without a splash of vodka, I headed back to the lab to find Jaime. The college was quiet, the hallways empty. We barely had time to process the fact that there were vampires in our world. I could only imagine what the college residents were going through, but I was glad to learn that Will and Kiki had told them what we had seen. They were both likeable and easy to believe. I was beginning to notice that it was a trait many Hamletville survivors seemed to have.

I pushed open the outside door and breathed in the morning air. It was good that Jaime was so preoccupied. The loss of Ian was hard to take. Memories of him standing on the beach, my shashka in his hand, clouded my mind. That's how I wanted to remember him, a hero who had saved us. The thing that Rumor had transformed him into was not his doing. Just like me, he had been fooled. He never even knew they were pumping vampire blood into him. It hadn't been a choice. It had been a manipulation.

Looking across the lawn, I scanned for the fox I'd seen the day before. There was nothing. I pulled my vest around me tighter and headed toward the doctor's lab. The hallway was quiet. I pushed the door open to find the lab empty. Doctor Gustav had abducted my man—again. On a table in the middle of the room was the body of the female vampire. Her corpse-like face was uncovered, but her body was hidden by a sheet. On another gurney beside her were the remains of the male vampire, such as they were.

I turned to go then paused a moment. The day before, the undead man hadn't spoke, but I had heard something. I was tired, but it didn't hurt to try again. I crossed the room to the closed door. On the other side, no doubt, the undead man was chained to his pole. It still unnerved me, and something about it nagged at me. It seemed wrong.

"Hello?" I called with my mind.

There was no noise from inside.

"Am I just hearing things, then? Can you hear me?"

Again, nothing, but a moment later from a closed door a few doors down, I heard a muffled word that sounded like someone had said *"fool."*

I looked around the lab. There was no one. Pausing to listen for any noise in the hallway, I realized I was totally alone. Except, I had heard something. There were four more doors along the wall. I went to the first one, and moving carefully, I slowly opened the door. Inside was a closet with row after row of bottles and other supplies. I closed the door quietly and moved forward toward what looked like an even larger room. My senses were on edge.

"Hello?"

Again, I heard a disgusted *"humph"* in reply.

I tried the door. It was unlocked. I pushed it open. Inside, ultraviolet light was glowing. And across the room, locked in what looked like a cage, was an undead woman. There was a metal sign on the cage that read, "Hazardous Materials Drain." On the floor of the cage was a drain. The cage itself was small, maybe no more than five feet in length and width. Inside, the undead woman stood perfectly still, watching me as I entered. Her silent, white eyes took in my every movement. I pulled my sword. Behind the gate, she couldn't possibly be a threat. And there was enough chain around the gate to keep a small army shackled in, but there was something menacing about her that I'd felt just a few times before: at the football field, in Rumor's suite, and once before in Hamletville when the undead piano virtuoso had lost his hand.

Trying to control my breathing, I eyed the room. There was another small closet just off the room, not apparent from the lab outside. I tried to sense if there was anything, or anyone, inside. I felt something, but I wasn't sure what. I looked back at the undead woman. Her skin was light gray, almost tipped blue along the edges. Her eyes were that same milk-white with streaks of red that I'd grown accustomed to. She did not froth at the mouth as many of the others had. She wore the remains of a blue nightgown, the bottom of the long gown torn and bloody. Her hair was dark and fell in messy, caked-up bunches across her chest. She studied me.

"You hear me, don't you?" I asked with my mind.

The undead woman tilted her head and looked at me, but she did not reply.

"What are you?" I asked.

After a long pause, I heard a reply echo through my head. *"You."*

I swallowed hard, my heart slamming in my chest. I was unsure what to say then. Should I ask why they were eating us? Should I ask what happened to her? *"What do you want?"*

"Out."

"So you can eat everyone alive?"

"No," an exasperated voice said in reply. And then, surprising me, she pointed at the closet nearby. *"There,"* she said.

I looked back at the closet. There was something in there, but what? Knowing Doctor Gustav, she could have a whole horde of zombies in there. If I opened the door, they could all come tumbling out. But there was something the woman wanted. What was it?

I reached for the door handle. It was locked.

"Locked," I said, looking at the undead woman.

A strange look of frustration crossed her face, and a deep angry growl rolled out of her as she slammed her hands in frustration against the cage. It was then that I noticed that one of her hands was deeply wounded, small cuts covering the back of her hands and fingers. She groaned deeply then set her head against the bars.

My heart racing, I stepped closer and looked at her.

From under a heavy lock of matted hair, she looked up at me with dead eyes. *"The doctor. The key."*

Just then, I heard the door open followed by the sound of Jaime's voice. "The lab door is open."

"Whose there?" I heard Doctor Gustav call, her voice filled with irritation.

"It's Layla," I replied then turned toward the door. I looked back at the undead woman who wore the expression of extreme frustration. She howled and slammed herself against the wall, marring her forehead.

"Layla, help me."

A shiver went down my spine.

"You found Mrs. Frankenstein," the doctor said. "She's a puzzle. Dangerous beast."

The undead woman hissed and snapped at the doctor.

"Best come out of there. She ripped out a handful of my hair the last time I tried to tangle with her. But I'll get a sample out of her yet."

I looked back at the woman who growled low and dangerous at the doctor.

"I'll come back," I told her.

The undead woman did not respond.

With shaking hands, I closed the door behind me. My head suddenly started to ache. "What...what are you working on?" I asked, seeing the doctor and Jaime setting down cases.

The doctor opened her case to reveal what looked like a number of torture devices.

"What the hell is that?" I asked.

Jaime shifted uncomfortably.

I eyed the cases over. Inside the box, I saw a sticker with the word's "Mister Iago's History of Torture Show. Great Expectations Carnival" written on the inside.

"I'm attempting to see what kind of pain tolerance these creatures have," the doctor said. "I've finally gathered enough solar energy to get an EEG reading. I need to see what, if anything, trips their senses. One of the last communications from the CDC said there was brain activity in the undead. I need to see what that looks like."

"Not on her," I said suddenly, motioning to the undead woman.

Both Jaime and the doctor looked up at me.

"Interesting, isn't it?" the doctor said, fixing me with a hard stare, her blue eyes boring into me. "At first there seemed to be no difference between any of them. They were all just killing machines. Now, however, there seems to be some patterns of distinction between the undead. She almost seems intelligent," the doctor said then looked at me expectantly.

I glanced at Jaime who was also gazing at me, an inquisitive look on his face. "Almost," I agreed.

The doctor exhaled sharply. "Either way, I'll get a reading on them both and see what's going on."

"How in the world will you get them to be still long enough to try," I replied. "Even chained or penned in, it will be impossible to get them wired."

"That's what this is for," the doctor said then crossed the room to the large wooden box that was sitting in one corner. Unlatching it, she opened the box. Inside were a spindle, chains, and a pulley device. I knew at once what it was. We had several in the Smithsonian, but we never displayed them.

Such barbarous tools were from a dark era in mankind's history, one that shamed my spirit.

"The rack," I whispered.

"Yes," the doctor replied. "More effective than just a gurney. This way we can completely subdue the subject."

"Victim seems more apt," I replied.

The doctor snorted in reply. "Now you sound like Tristan. You didn't seem to have any qualms with ethics last night."

"That was different."

"Why?"

"Because they meant to do us harm. They had to be exposed."

"And these creatures don't? Last night you killed a living creature. I don't even plan to kill my test subjects, just learn about them. Which is worse? Don't be a hypocrite."

"I—" I began, but Jaime cut in.

"The vampires we encountered were vicious, bloodthirsty. Layla was trying to protect us. She didn't want what happened to some of our people to happen here."

Doctor Gustav nodded. "I respect that. But people in glass houses..." she said, her voice trailing off. "Now, there is a lot of work to do. Will you be staying?" she asked, turning to me.

"No, I won't."

"Jaime?" the doctor asked.

"Maybe we can learn something good here, Layla," he told me. "The doctor is very close. She believes she may know what caused it."

"If only I could test my theory on something other than rats," the doctor muttered under her breath.

I shook my head. "I don't know about this, Jaime."

Jaime looked torn. "Layla, I…"

"Okay, but meet me around lunch time?" I finally relented.

He looked relieved.

Mrs. Frankenstein. For some reason, the doctor's moniker for the undead woman set my teeth on edge.

LAYLA

I wandered slowly back toward the main area of the college. My mind was bent on the undead woman. I wasn't hearing things. She really had spoken to me. What in the world did that mean? I hated Doctor Gustav's experiments, but she was right about one thing. The undead woman did seem — and was — intelligent. All along they'd just seemed like mindless flesh-eaters. But that wasn't the case at all. The more rotted ones didn't seem to have any awareness of their humanity anymore. But the others were something different.

I passed a few people in the hallway, college survivors I recognized from the night before. I didn't want to meet their eyes. God knows what they thought.

"Hey, Layla, right?" a woman asked.

I stopped, smiled. The woman was about my age. She had on jeans and an old Penn State sweatshirt, her hair pulled back into a ponytail.

"Thank you for what you did last night. Will and Kiki...they said you saw those things before?"

"Unfortunately, yes."

"So they always existed," the woman more stated than said.

"I never saw one before this week," I replied. After everything that had happened, it seemed like life in Hamletville was eons ago. In reality, barely a week had passed.

"What should we do now?"

"Keep our eyes and ears open. But there is holy water here. Maybe someone could cork some up and make sure everyone gets some."

"I can do that," the woman said then stuck out her hand. "I'm Gwen."

"Nice to meet you."

"Everyone is grateful for what you did. People are just spooked. Let me know if I can do anything, okay?"

I nodded.

I had originally thought to head to the Student Union, to talk to the others, but I just wasn't ready. Instead, I dodged down a side hallway between the classrooms and exited the building at the back. On the back lawn, I spotted an enormous oak tree. I went to it and sat down. The branches overhead had the first buds of spring. The new leaves were just about ready to burst out. I tipped my head against the oak and closed my eyes. It was quiet outside. In the distance, I could hear men talking. Must have been the guards at the gate. Their words were muffled. Overhead, songbirds called. From somewhere in the forest behind the college, I could hear frogs singing. Given it was morning, the sun was still hidden by the mist rising off the lake. It wouldn't be until later in the day that the fog cleared. A breeze swept across the grounds, shifting the branches overhead.

I must have fallen asleep then because I woke later with a thin layer of morning dew wetting my hair and skin. I heard someone approaching me. Startled, I jumped up, my hand on the hilt of my sword.

To my great relief, it was Tristan.

"I come in peace," he said, raising his hands. "Something tells me you were the kind of child who liked to climb trees."

"How did you know?"

Tristan walked over to the large oak, grabbed a low branch, and pulled himself up. "Well, Peryn's ward, what are you waiting for?" he asked then climbed further into the tree, dropping over the back side of the fence.

This will be interesting. I grabbed a branch, pulled myself upward, then followed. The bark felt gritty in my hands, but I kept my grasp tight and moved across the branches and over the side of the fence. I then swung down and dropped to the forest floor. Tristan reached out to steady me.

"Now, off to Baba Yaga's house, or do you have a sparrow-drawn walnut for us to shrink down and ride in?" I asked him with a grin.

"More like the first. And, second, I'm not *that* kind of fairy."

"All right," I said with a laugh. "Where are we headed?"

"You'll see," he replied then led me into the forest.

It was calm and peaceful under the trees. The hemlocks shimmered green. The first snowdrops dotted the forest floor with petite white flowers. Newborn ferns unfurled their long fingers. I looked Tristan over as I walked and questioned myself. There I went again just trusting someone. Once more I was being led off by a being from the other world without rhyme or reason. Hadn't I learned my lesson the first time?

"What are you?" I asked Tristan.

"I'm like Peryn."

"Who are the fox people?"

"The unseelie, the kitsune...they have a lot of names. But they hate you, and us, that is certain."

"Why?"

"The unseelie stayed in this realm when mankind became barbarous. They are, after all, earth spirits. It is their job to protect the earth, to keep watch over nature. Mankind has finally brought Mother Nature to her knees. If you continued on the way you have, the planet would die. They saw only one solution."

"To kill us."

"Yes."

"A fox woman led us into a trap. We passed through a kind of labyrinth that took us from the hotel, where we fought the vampires, to the woods where Cricket found us. We walked into a horde of zombies."

"The vampires are the ancient enemy of all our kind...both the seelies and the unseelies. It is said that once, long ago, the vampires and my kind were one race. What happened to divide us is now lost to lore, but the vampires hate all earth spirits."

"Did the unseelies...the kitsune...plan to turn us into monsters?"

"No, they planned to kill you. It was foretold they would cause mankind's demise. They are trying to decimate you. The kitsune you encountered was very clever. She killed you and the vampires all in one shot."

"The vampire woman said we killed their queen."

"You've cut off the snake's head. The nightwalkers have barely held on. They cannot survive this. They cannot feed on the undead, and the living are too few. And if they all fight like you do, then their days are surely numbered."

We came to a line of boulders on the hilltop. There was a wide gap between the rocks, a passage in the very center of boulders. Mountain laurel and other scrub covered the hilltop. A wind blew from the gap between boulders. It was warm, sweet, and smelled of flowers.

"You came to the forest by traveling through one of the many thin places in this world. There are old, magical passages that can move you through space in the blink of an eye. Such places are known to the seelie and unseelie. While my kind lives in the otherworld, we occasionally venture into your world," Tristan said, motioning to the boulders.

I stared at the passage. "Would the surviving humans be welcomed in your world?"

"Perhaps. But not yet."

"Why not?"

"Because shadows still loom."

"What should I do? What do you—does Peryn—want me to do?"

"Save the innocent."

Tristan turned and began walking back toward the college. After a moment, however, he stopped. "Race you to the wall?" he asked. He grinned at me, and a moment later, he was engulfed in shimmering golden light that blinded me, forcing me to close my eyes. When I opened them again, I saw a dog sitting where Tristan had been. He wagged his tail, gave a happy muffled bark, and then dashed back toward the college.

I cast a glance back at the dark passage. I swore I heard a child's laughter echo from the space, followed by the scent of flowers and the feel of sunlight. Save the innocent. For some terrifying reason, I was beginning to suspect that Tristan hadn't meant just the living.

LAYLA

That night, the Hamletville survivors met with the others in the union for dinner. I had to smile when I saw Kira and Susan playing tag with the other children, all of them laughing loudly.

As I ate canned green beans, hash, and jellybeans off a cafeteria tray, I watched Gwen, the girl I had met earlier that day, and Kellimore circulate the room passing out plastic rosary beads and small beakers filled with holy water.

"I like them," Summer said as she pushed her green beans from one side of her plate to the other. "They seem to be good people," she added then began motioning to the table across from ours with her fork. "Daycare worker, hairstylist, mechanic, bicycle shop owner, receptionist, YMCA swim instructor…just regular people like us. But we've been lucky. Ariel and Darius had a grizzly story to tell, as did many of the others. We got lucky in Hamletville, at least for a while." She sighed and forked her green beans. She grimaced when she took a bite.

"They can't be that bad," I said, eating a bite. They were. They were pickled green beans. "God, you'd think I made them."

Summer laughed. "Hey, there's Jaime."

Jaime entered, Doctor Gustav following behind him. I smiled at him and waved him over. He exchanged words with the doctor then joined us.

"There you are," I said, rising. I kissed him, gazing deeply at his face. He looked tired, and he'd changed his shirt. He was wearing a deep-green Claddagh-Basel College T-shirt. "How did it go?"

"Grizzly," he said, "but we got a test started," he said, casting a side-long glance at Summer.

"Sit. I'll get you something," I told him.

"That's okay," he replied. "I can get it."

"I'm no little woman" I said with a laugh, "but I love you, and you look tired. Sit."

Acquiescing, Jaime took a spot beside Summer. When I reached the food table, I found Kellimore there. He handed me a rosary and a vial of holy water.

"Talked to Gwen," he said. "Good idea. You know, you're pretty badass with that thing," he said, motioning to the sword.

"Thanks. I was a state champ in fencing. Almost went to the Olympics."

"No kidding?" he replied, then that haunted look crossed his face again. "Anyway, thanks again for last night...Buffy," he said with a laugh then wandered off.

Ms. Katana and now Buffy. Nice. I filled a plate for Jaime and headed back to the table. Jaime was talking with Will and Tom while Ethel kept Kiki's and Frenchie's attention pointing out all the men in the room she thought were worth their time, including Tristan who was sitting elbow to elbow with Cricket. I chuckled to myself, wondering what her reaction would be if I told her that he was actually a dog.

"I worked the perimeter of the college today," Buddie told me. "The fence is in good shape, just a couple of small cracks at the base. Otherwise, that fence could withstand a huge undead assault."

"So, then it's just the vampires, fox women, and Mad Max types we need to worry about," I replied.

"They've been doing well here until recently," Will said.

"Until we showed up," Tom corrected.

"It's not our fault. We just brought the bad news with us," Will said.

"I don't think anywhere is really safe anymore," Summer said.

I thought about the passage between the rocks. "Maybe," I said absently.

"The doctor has been running some tests," Jaime said then. "In a couple more weeks, we might have an answer."

"Like a cure?" Summer asked.

Jaime nodded. "She's closing the gaps at both ends, what caused it and what can cure it. She's close."

"Layla, can you imagine?" Summer said. "Maybe we'll have a fighting chance. We are going to stay here awhile, aren't we?"

I realized then that everyone in the Hamletville group had stopped talking and were looking at me. I cast a glance back at Tristan. He had taken Cricket by the chin and kissed her on the nose, making her giggle. "Yes. But that doesn't mean we'll be perfectly safe," I said, casting a look at Jaime, "but we might have a chance. Better than on the open road."

"Yeah. Road to nowhere," Will said with a laugh.

He was right. If we did leave now, where would we go?

Back in the library, Jaime and I lay cuddled together looking up at the stars. Moonlight shimmered in through the window. When it grew dark, many of the college survivors, and Ethel and Summer, had all gone to the college chapel. With Pastor Frank gone, there were no holy men left, but Ethel had run enough church socials and fundraisers that she figured she knew how to do some good. It was nice to see her busy with something. Tom had gone back to Baker Street, curling up with Holmes in the opposite corner of the library. Buddie and Will went out to help the watch, Elle introduced Frenchie and the girls to the art studio, and Kiki had gone off with the doctor.

"We got the male undead strapped in and started getting some readings off him," Jaime told me.

"What did you find?"

"There is some brain activity there. Doctor Gustav was going to have Kiki help her mark the readings tonight."

"Did you see the undead woman?"

"Just for a minute."

"And?"

"She's different from the others."

"Yes," I replied, "she is." I rolled over and looked at Jaime.

He leaned forward and placed a sweet kiss on my lips. His mouth was warm and soft and he tasted like licorice jellybeans.

"I love you," he whispered, stroking my hair away from my face.

"I love you too," I replied, pulling him in for another kiss, and then another. My hands stroked his strong back and under his shirt, feeling his flesh. More than anything, I wanted to feel that flesh against mine one more time. I pulled his shirt up and over his head then let my hands graze down his chest, sitting up to kiss his neck, my lips sliding down his chest. Jaime pulled off my shirt and I deftly unhooked my bra, tossing it to the side. It felt so nice, so natural to have his hands on me. Jaime was so careful, gentle in the way he touched me. He touched me like he loved me, and I loved that about him.

"Layla," he whispered in my ear as he gently stroked his hands down my bare back. He unbuttoned my jeans, and soon we were both sliding off the rest of our clothes. Jaime lay down as I drizzled kisses down his chest, his stomach. And then we fell into each other, a blur of flesh and feeling and love overwhelming us both.

LAYLA

"We're looking for Layla." Chase's voice rising from the common area of the library woke me.

"She's still asleep, honey. What's the matter?" Ethel replied.

"Well," I heard Cricket begin, then heard her pause, "some folks went into town earlier today and haven't come back. Doc wants us to go have a look. Thought it might be a good idea to have Layla come along."

I rose groggily and went to the door. Jaime was gone. No doubt he'd taken pity on me, letting me sleep. "I'm awake," I called. "Give me five minutes?"

"Sure thing," Cricket called.

"Ethel, where's Buddie?" I asked.

"Sleeping, I think," she replied, motioning to the study room where Buddie was bunked.

Wiping sleep from my eyes, I crossed the room and knocked on Buddie's door. "Want to go for a jog?" I called to the closed door.

Buddie opened the door. He was already dressed and adjusting his quiver. "Ready when you are."

I looked over my shoulder at Cricket and Chase who had passed a glance to one another. "Buddie is a good tracker," I called to them.

"All right then," Cricket replied.

Ten minutes later, Chase, Cricket, Buddie, and I were at the front gate.

"How long they been gone?" Cricket asked the guards.

"About three hours. Should have been a half-hour trip, but," Joe said, casting a glance at me, "I saw the second group pass down Main about an hour after they went out."

"Second group of what?" I asked, feeling my heartbeat quicken.

"Two trucks," the man replied. "And a horde following them."

I looked at Cricket, and a sick feeling washed over me. "Cricket, who's out there?"

Cricket pulled a pistol from the back of her jeans and checked her ammo. Then, from a bag strapped around her shoulder, she pulled out a box of ammo and handed it to me. It was for my magnum.

"Kellimore, Elle...and Jaime."

I felt my heart drop to my stomach.

"We'll go slow and quiet," Chase said. "If we need to come back and get every gun in this place, we will. But let's see what's going on first."

"Kellimore could have them all hidden in a damned treehouse for all we know," Cricket added.

"Where's Tristan?" I asked.

Cricket frowned. "He's not here right now."

Now it was my turn to frown. I looked at Buddie.

"Let's go," he said.

It must have been near noon. The languid fog was rising slowly off the lake. It was deadly silent. Rather than going by street, we took to the backyards all along the hillside and headed in the direction Joe had indicated. No one breathed. Cricket held fast to her big wrench as we moved from house to house, all our ears working hard to pick up on the slightest sound. We moved carefully. We were about to round the back of a garage when Buddie reached out and pulled Cricket to a stop. He motioned for all of us to be quiet and get low.

Buddie tapped his ear, and we all listened. In the distance, we heard vehicle doors slam followed by the popping sound of gunfire.

My hands started shaking. Jaime.

We ran behind the hair salon. As we were rushing, I swore I saw someone standing in the driveway of one of the houses. A woman...with red hair. When I looked back, my heart froze. Sitting in the grass was a fox. It looked at me, swished its tail, and then darted off into the underbrush. Dammit! Tristan was right. The kitsune were up to no good, and this time they had struck at my very heart. For a moment, fear gripped me and I shuddered, but I remembered something my grandma used to tell me: *My Layla, if your eyes are afraid, let your hands do the work.*

I gripped my shashka tighter.

Moving carefully, Chase led us to a three-story house sitting at the edge of the mountain where it curved northward. Motioning to us, we followed him onto the back porch. He lifted the welcome mat, grabbed a key, and then unlocked the back door. We went inside. The air inside the house had a flat, stale smell. Lace doilies covered every table. Prim needlepoints of flowers, photos of children, grandchildren, weddings, proms, and family reunions covered the walls. When we turned to go upstairs, however, I found something else on the wall: a massive spray of blood.

"What the hell?" I said.

"Yeah, they cleaned this place before we got here. Guess it was a rough go. Someone from the college early on got bit, but it's clear now. And it's got a hell of a view of the town from the attic," Chase said then led us upstairs.

We followed quietly behind him.

"Why were Jaime and the others out?" I asked Cricket.

She shook her head. "Doc said they went on a supply run, just like we did the other day. She wanted some parts from the hardware store."

"I thought Tristan told her no more runs," I replied.

Cricket nodded. "The doc don't mind too well."

"She'll hear from me this time."

"She's due for a good lecture."

The attic of the house smelled like asbestos and dust. The old door opened with a creak. We went to the window. Chase reached out to lift the blind but Buddie stopped him.

"See, don't be seen," Buddie cautioned him.

Chase nodded.

Cricket pulled a pair of binoculars from her bag and handed it to Chase. He cracked the blind just a little and peered out while Buddie went to look out the corner of the other window.

I went to the third window and looked out. The old house had a fabulous view of the entire town. You could clearly see the lake, most of the roads, including a good view the roads coming in and going out of town. I even spotted railroad tracks leading toward a dark train tunnel. In the yard below was a massive tree. And sitting under that tree was the fox. It sat looking up at us. Dammit again. She was going to lead them right to us.

"There," Buddie said, "the YMCA."

I joined Buddie at the window. In the distance, I saw several trucks parked outside the YMCA. People were all over the place. Some were going in and out of the building. Others were shooting some of the undead. But two more were luring the horde of at least three dozen zombies into the gated basketball court.

"There's Kellimore," Chase said. "He's in the back of the truck. Face is busted up. They've got his hands tied."

I squinted, and saw a man with a rifle lift Kellimore to his feet then push him out of the back of a truck. He fell to his knees. Jaime jumped out behind him and helped him up. Two other men were dragging Elle along. I saw one of the men stick his hand between her legs. Elle kicked and pulled away only to get slapped. When Jaime reached out for her, another shoved him to the ground. Kicking and fighting, they dragged Elle into the building.

My heart froze. Something deep and dark inside me looked out. My body trembled as rage overtook me.

"Maybe eight or so...living. Looks like they got the undead corralled. Not killing them though," Chase said as he watched. "Look. They're just locking them in."

"We can go back," Cricket said. "We can get some help."

"Good idea," I told her. "You three go. I'll stay here and keep watch. If they head this way, I'll hurry back."

Buddie turned and looked at me as if to say he did not believe, not even for a minute, that I would stay put. "I'll stay with you," he told me somberly, but his tone told me more. He would stay with me, and he would help me with whatever it was I planned to do next.

"All right," I replied.

Cricket laughed. "Darlin', you may be a lot of things, but you're no poker player. What's the plan?"

"Ah, hell no," Chase said then shook his head, but I couldn't help but notice he was grinning. "Can't we wait until dark at least?"

"Vampires come out in the dark," I reminded him.

"Don't you remember what happened at the Big Wheel?" Cricket said to him.

"I sure do."

"They'll rape Elle ten times by then and probably kill her and the others," I replied. I looked outside once more. The fox was gone. I started loading my magnum. "We need to go now."

24
LAYLA

Moving quietly and keeping low, we headed toward the YMCA. The fog was still thick enough that it gave us some cover. My heart was thundering in my chest. I needed to get to Jaime. If anything happened to Jaime, I didn't know what I'd do. And from the look of Kellimore's face, I needed to do something fast.

We moved down the railroad tracks, turning and cutting across the back lawn of a daycare center. Nearby, and directly across from the YMCA, was a field with very tall, dry grass. Buddie motioned for us to move into the grass.

The hair on the back of my neck rose. Cricket and Chase darted into the grass. I scanned the horizon. Something was off here. I looked back to see the fox sitting on the railroad tracks.

"There," I whispered to Buddie, pointing at the fox. "Shoot that bitch."

Buddie followed my hand. "The fox?"

"That's no fox."

Buddie nocked an arrow, aimed, and let it fly.

Moving fast, the fox turned and trotted down the tracks toward the train tunnel.

"Trouble is coming," I whispered.

"Coming? Everything feels wrong. Like we're being watched."

I nodded, then, ducking low, Buddie and I followed Chase and Cricket onto the field. We made our way toward the road. Soon I could hear the sound of rough voices coming from inside the YMCA, as well as the groans of the undead who they'd pinned up outside.

"Tony," I heard a male voice call. Getting low, I spied them through the long grass. A rough looking man about fifty years old, a shotgun hanging over his shoulder, was talking to a man sitting on the bench beside the basketball court. "Take Jones and scout around. These three look pretty comfy. Figure out where they're holing up, and we'll get the herd ready for dinner. Hear that, rotters? Dinner time is coming," the man said then threw a bottle over the fence into the group of the undead who hissed and bit at the man. He laughed and went back inside. The door, I noticed, remained open about an inch or so.

I scanned the horde of the undead. They were, for the most part, rotting corpses. At the back of the pack was a large undead man who was not hissing and biting. Instead, he was staring at the grass, at us.

"Ugly fucking pets," Tony said as he made faces at the undead, mimicking their actions.

Tony then went to the open door of the YMCA, whistled, and a moment later another well-armed man joined him. They set off in one of the trucks. It wouldn't take them long to find the college. While we outnumbered them, it didn't mean that we could easily fight thinking men and a horde that size...a horde these men were using as their own personal hit squad. Well, turnabout was fair play.

I eyed the compound. The glass front door had been propped open. Inside, I saw a large reception area. Behind that, I saw the open equipment room. It was hard to see what was happening, but people were moving around inside.

"Ideas?" Buddie whispered.

"That gate locked?" I whispered to Chase who pulled out a pair of binoculars.

"No, just closed with a chain wrapped around it."

I looked back at the undead man. He'd now come to the fence and was looking out at us.

"Can you hear me?" I whispered with my mind.

I watched as he scanned the grass looking for me. After a few moments, a reply came. *"Yes."*

"Are those gasoline cans in the back of that truck?" Cricket asked.

"Sure are. And I do have a lighter," Chase said with a grin.

"We need to get the men out of the building. Buddie, go around back and see if you can get in from there. Be ready to grab our people. Chase and Cricket, spark up those gas cans and blow up one of their trucks. Then run like hell. Meet us at the blue house."

"Why? What are you going to do?"

"I'm going to feed them," I said, motioning to the undead.

"You sure that's wise, letting them out?" Buddie asked.

I wasn't, but I was certain that I could solicit some help. I nodded.

"Ready?" I asked.

Moving low, we raced across the street. Buddie disappeared behind the building while Chase and Cricket headed to the farthest truck. I went to the side of the building across from the basketball court, slipping in between two soda machines. I paused, took a deep breath, and then pulled my shashka.

"She looks like a lezzie," I heard one of the men say. "Hey, lezzie, you ever fuck a man before?"

"No. Have you?" I heard Elle reply.

The sound of a sharp smack followed.

"Get your hands off her," Jaime shouted.

"Shut the hell up or I'll fuck you next," a man replied.

I then heard the muffled sound of Jaime cursing as someone, it seemed, gagged him.

I stared at the undead horde across from me. They could see me, smell me. Up close, they were a terrible sight. Many of them had been burned. Their hair, clothing, and skin was singed. The smell wafting off of them was so horrid that it nearly took my breath away. They snapped and bit at me. Some of their milky white eyes had begun to take on a yellow sheen. And I noticed that one of them, in the corner, had fallen. His leg, broken apart at the knee, lay on the ground. They were little more than pulp and sinew. The undead man in the back, however, moved forward. The unthinking undead paid him little mind. His pants hung low around his emaciated waist, and he had a bruises all around his neck like someone had choked him to death. He was missing an ear on the left side of his head.

"You, you hear me." I said to him.

"Yes."

"Help me, and I'll set you free," I told him.

The undead man squinted hard at me. *"Help you?"*

"If I set you free, will you help me?"

"Set me free," the undead man seethed.

"You didn't exactly agree," I told him as I stepped closer to the gate, my sword in front of me.

He tilted his head to the side, those pale eyes watching me, tracking my movements. *"Yes,"* he said quietly.

Moving as quietly as I could, I unwound the chain from the gate. Then, I waited. A moment later, I heard a massive explosion from the other side of the building. Orange light flashed, illuminating the place. Another moment later, there was another explosion.

"What the fuck was that?" I heard one of the men shout.

"Jesus Christ, the truck is on fire!"

"Bill, let go of that girl and get out there."

Using my shashka, I lifted the bar on the gate. While the gate opened slowly, the mindless undead did not crowd the undead man who'd spoken to me. Rather, he held them back while I retreated toward the side door. I pulled it open, looking quickly inside. All the men were out front.

Then, the undead man rushed out of the basketball court toward the front of the building, the mindless rabble following him.

"How the fuck did they get out?" I heard one of the men yell followed by a blood-curdling scream.

I pulled the door closed behind me then turned and raced into the room. Buddie pushed open a back door and joined me in the equipment room. Through the open front door, I saw the horde of undead attacking the men who'd led them there. There was a firefight as the men, caught unaware, were overrun. The undead man who'd communicated with me stepped into the doorway. Then, he pulled the door closed, turned, and lunged toward one of the men. He moved with great speed, shoving him to the ground, and tearing into his throat with his teeth.

"Did you see that? He shut the door! What the fuck was that?" Elle said, aghast.

"No time to explain," I said, turning to her. She'd been bound to one of the pieces of gym equipment. Her shirt had been ripped open, the buttons snapped off, her bra cut at the middle. "You...you okay?" I whispered to her as I untied her.

Across the room, Buddie untied Jaime and Kellimore.

"I'm going to kill every one of those mother fuckers," she said then.

"You don't have to."

From outside, we heard screaming. The sound of gunfire seemed to slow and then we heard it no more. A moment later, however, I heard the screech of tires, and someone yelling. "Jesus Christ, who let the rotters out? What the...Run! They're all dead! Run!"

"Let's go," Buddie said and we all headed to the back door.

Moving quietly, we headed out the back of the building to the street below. Just in case my unnatural alliance was about to fall apart, I didn't want to go back to the college.

"The big blue house," I told Kellimore, who I noticed was limping, as we moved across town.

"This way," he said, leading us back toward Main Street.

Moving fast, we rushed across the road. The undead were not looking in our direction. We moved quickly, cutting across lawns and parking lot, to the house. Cricket and Chase were waiting inside. They opened the door for us, pulled us in, and then locked the door behind us. Cricket led Kellimore, Jaime, and Elle to the living room while Chase and Buddie ran back upstairs to the attic. I went to the landing on the second floor and looked out. The undead were milling around in front of the YMCA, seemingly unsure what to do. And the thinking undead man, some kind of odd ghoul—not vampire, not zombie—was looking toward the train tunnel where the fox had disappeared. It almost seemed like he was waiting. For what, I didn't know. But the thought unnerved me.

LAYLA

Elle passed me on the stairs. She went into one of the bedrooms. I followed her. When I got to the doorway, I saw her standing in front of an open closet. She dashed away a tear. "You okay?" I whispered.

She nodded.

"Can I do anything for you?"

She shook her head. "I just...I just need a minute."

"Please let me know if I can do anything," I said then pulled the door closed.

From behind the closed door, I heard a soft sob. It broke my heart. Thank God we had gotten there in time, but just in time. Still, she'd had to face unwanted hands on her. It was a grotesque horror. I tried not to think about what Ian had done to me after the vampire blood had transformed him.

I went back to the living room where Cricket was looking over Kellimore. "Well, they sure messed up your pretty face," she told him.

Though it pained him, he smiled at her.

"Let me see if I can find anything to get you guys cleaned up, then we need to get back. The undead are still milling around down there. We need to get out of sight before they find us," I told them then headed toward the kitchen.

I opened cupboard after cupboard. They were bare. Even the small washroom just off the kitchen had been cleared out. There was, however, a large closet just across from the back door. There, I found a stroller parked and folded up. Beside it was a diaper bag. Inside, I found several changes of baby clothes, diapers, spit cloths, bottled water, wipes, and a good-sized medicine kit. Inside it I found an emergency ice pack. I went back to the parlor and started pulling out supplies. I snapped a cold pack in half and handed it to Kellimore. "Press that on your eyes. Keep switching it out."

"Where'd you find all that?" Kellimore asked.

I poured a little water onto one of the spit cloths and began mopping up the nasty cut above Jaime's eye. "Diaper bag. Moms are always prepared."

Jaime winced but didn't complain.

"Doesn't need stitches," I told him. "Just looks a mess." After I had cleaned up the cut, I dabbed a little antibacterial cream on it then bandaged it.

"Hurts like hell," he said then looked at me. His gaze spoke volumes. It was all I could do to keep myself from folding him into my arms and weeping uncontrollably. I'd almost lost him. It was too horrible to consider, so I didn't. It seemed all I did anymore was shut down my feelings. What was going to happen if I kept bottling everything up inside? I exhaled deeply, shook my head, and smiled softly at him.

He returned my look with a mirrored *can you believe this shit* expression.

I took the ice pack from Kellimore and handed it to Jaime. "Put this on your cheek," I told him then began working on Kellimore. "Who lived here?" I asked as I scanned the photos on the wall.

"Mr. and Mrs. Stone," Kellimore said, motioning to a photo on the wall of an old, white-haired couple. "They owned the Ford garage."

"Who had the baby?" I scanned the room to see a photo lying on the coffee table. I picked it up. In the image was a smiling woman holding a pretty little baby that looked to be no more than one or two months old. The photo had been taken outside. The woman's dark hair was glimmering in the sunlight, and leaves on the trees behind her were hues of red and orange.

"The Stones had a daughter, Elizabeth. She babysat me once or twice when I was a kid. I think I remember seeing her around during Autumn Leaf Festival…right before everything went to hell. Mr. Stone was one of the first ones to get sick."

I motioned to the blood stain on the wall. "What happened there?"

"I don't know. I didn't clean this end of town. Doctor Gustav came here with a group. They got overrun. One of the people she was with got bit. Don't know what happened to the Stones. We used this place later because it's a good lookout."

"What happened to the person who got bit?"

"Doc gave them a lethal dose of something."

"But what about after?"

"After?"

"After they…you know, after they came back as one of the undead?"

"Oh," Kellimore said. "I don't know. She took care of it, I guess."

I looked at the woman in the picture. Something about her seemed vaguely familiar. Had she worked in DC? I stuck the photo in my pocket.

A moment later, the back door opened and Tristan, Joe, Darius, and Will entered.

"Cricket?" Tristan called.

"Here. We're here," she yelled in reply.

"Are you all right?" he asked her then looked at the rest of us.

"We're okay. They got banged up a bit, but they're all right," she told him.

"Where's Elle?" he asked.

"Upstairs," I replied.

"I'll go check on her," Cricket said then disappeared up the stairs.

I sat down on the couch beside Jaime, took his hand, and kissed it. I hated seeing him so broken. I was sick of everyone I loved being battered around.

"How'd they nab you?" Tristan asked.

"We were coming out of the hardware store when they drove up on us. We didn't even see them until it was too late. All of a sudden there were guns on us, and that horde was following behind them. It was like they were trailing that horde along with them like pets," Jaime said.

Tristan stood, listening, with his arms folded across his chest.

"How'd you get free?" Will asked.

Jaime motioned to me.

"Diversion," I answered.

"We saw that diversion from the gate. All of a sudden there was a tower of orange flame leaping up in the middle of town," Joe said.

"Cricket and Chase blew up some gas cans, caught a truck on fire. Their pets turned on them and finished the job."

"And where are those pets now?" Tristan asked.

"They were still there," I said, "in front of the YMCA."

"There's a good view from the attic," Kellimore said then moved to stand up.

"Whoa," I told him, sitting him back down. "Give it a minute, big guy."

Tristan nodded then turned to head upstairs. But he paused for a moment first, turning to look at Kellimore. "Why were you out?"

"Doc sent us on a run," Kellimore said. "Dammit, I dropped the stuff she sent me after in front of the hardware store."

Tristan scowled, his golden eyes narrowing. He was about to head upstairs when Chase's voice echoed through the house.

"We gotta move," he screamed. "Everyone! Now! We gotta move!"

I ran to the second floor landing window and looked out. There, coming out of the railroad tunnel, was the largest horde of the undead I'd ever seen.

CRICKET

Chase's voice rattled down the stairwell to the bedroom where Elle and I were sitting. She'd just finished getting redressed. My heart broke for her. Seemed like just about every girl I ever knew had been subjected to some man putting his hands on her in a way she didn't want. Why was it that men always wanted to grab what wasn't theirs? I didn't have much time to think it over more because I knew from the tone in Chase's voice, we were in trouble.

Tristan pushed open the door. "Let's go," he told us, and we headed to the back of the house.

"Quiet. Go low and quiet," Buddie, Layla's friend, told us. I liked Buddie. He was probably my dad's age. He reminded me a lot of the guys from the carnival, bless their souls. He knew his stuff. Like Vella, his eyes were always canvasing the place. He saw more than other people. And I could see that Layla trusted him.

With her arm around her man, her sword pulled, Layla and the others headed out first while Darius helped Kellimore who was badly limping, the others following them. Tristan and I brought up the rear. We moved quickly across town.

"There," Kellimore whispered. "There is a closed rolling gate along the train tracks down on Fifth Street. If we stay low, they won't see us."

We made our way quick and easy. Only once did I catch a glimpse of what Chase had seen, and it scared the hell out of me. There were hundreds of zombies coming out of that train tunnel.

"Where'd they come from?" I whispered to Tristan.

"It's a siege," he replied. "Someone led them here."

"Those men?"

Tristan shook his head. "Someone else."

"They can't break down the walls, can they? They can't get through?

Tristan took my hand, kissed it, but said nothing. No answer was definitely not a good answer.

We crossed the railroad tracks, keeping low, then headed up the hill toward the college. It was dead silent. The mist had lifted. It was sunny and quiet. Not even the birds were chirping. Weird. We reached the college without anyone seeing us. The guards at the gate were about to call out when Tristan stepped forward and motioned for them to be quiet. He then ushered everyone through the gate.

"Get everyone inside," Tristan told Chase. "Start spreading the word that we are on lockdown. Be sure they move quickly and quietly. Silence is our greatest weapon."

"On it," Chase said and he and the others headed into the college.

"What can I do?" Layla asked. I could see from the look on her face that she wanted to help, but her eyes kept going to her man.

"You've done so much already. Jaime needs rest. Get your people ready," Tristan told her.

She gave him a knowing look, nodded, then they headed inside.

Something about what he said to her, the way he said it, made my stomach flop. Ready for what…other than zombies?

Tristan and I helped the guards lock down the gate then roll out the secondary metal gate. It would take a tank to push it down.

"Sweep the perimeter once more," Tristan told the two men on guard, "then come in the south entrance. Make sure everyone is inside. We'll lock the building down."

The men nodded then went on their way.

"I'm headed to see Doctor Gustav. It may get ugly—"

"I'm coming," I told him.

He raised an eyebrow at me. "You certain?"

"Oh, yeah, I wouldn't miss this for the life of me."

As I walked beside Tristan, who was moving like he had purpose, I remembered when my daddy and I came across Mister Marx, the carnival manager, getting read the riot act. A woman was screaming at him, telling him she'd been ripped off by our flea-bag circus. I was ready to fight in Mister Marx's defense, but my daddy told me to look and listen. It didn't take me long to understand that she was pointing out something important. Where did all that entrance money go? Marx was charging thirty dollars per person to get into the carnival—thirty per person. Sure as shootin', it wasn't lining our pockets. If you don't really look and listen, sometimes the important stuff slips right under your nose.

Tristan led us inside the doctor's wing, locking the outside door then pulling the metal accordion door closed behind it. We stopped again at a T in the hallway. Once again, Tristan rolled out the accordion gates and locked them. We'd set up all the barricades early as a backup in case of a breech. It scared me to see Tristan pulling out all the stops.

When he was done, we went to the doc's lab. Tristan pushed open the door, not bothering to knock. The doctor, who was looking into a microscope, looked up at us from behind her big glasses. She wore an annoyed expression on her face.

"The college is on lockdown," Tristan began abruptly. "No lights, no sounds, no anything. I've initiated the lockdown procedure. Chase is carrying it out since Kellimore is severely wounded."

"Wounded? How did—" the doc began but Tristan cut her off.

"There must be at least two hundred undead passing through. No one goes outside the building unless I say so. And this time, you will obey my order," Tristan told the doc who stood looking at him like a child caught with her hand in the cookie jar.

"Tristan, you know I never intend—" the doc began but Tristan cut her off again.

"It doesn't matter what you did and didn't intend. Two men are injured because you disobeyed my order. Now you will follow my word. No one goes outside for any reason. I've pulled the watch, rolled out the secondary gate. We are in a precarious situation, don't you understand? We're nearly surrounded. The only thing between the people in here and death are the walls. All the doors are being shuttered. We are being hunted. We need to stay out of sight. If we stay behind these walls, I have a better chance of keeping everyone safe."

"I wasn't trying to get anyone hurt or killed or anything else. How was I supposed to know this would happen? I'm just trying to stop this madness."

"Carla," Tristan said to her then, softening a bit. "You must understand. This cannot be stopped. This is mankind's endgame."

The doc glared at him, her lips pulling into a thin line. "What makes you so sure? Look," she said, picking up a vial. "This...this is the contaminant," she said, waving it in front of her. "And this," she added, picking up another tube, "is the cure! I've done it. All I need to do is run a test, but I know I've done it. I can see the results in the slides," she said, motioning to her microscope. "Don't tell me mankind has fallen."

"For just a moment, won't you put your work aside? We all need to be ready for what may come next."

"Come next?"

"Doc," I said then, jumping in. I hoped maybe she'd be able to take it better from me. "There are hundreds of zombies coming. If they find us, they might just get through. We may have to run."

The doc stared at her tables, her work, then back at Tristan and me. "All right. I'll go down to the union and get the emergency med packs ready," she said, defeated.

"And get rid of your pet," Tristan said, motioning to one of the closed doors along the wall. "We both know it's not safe. End it. I don't want anyone getting hurt if we end up in a mess of confusion."

The doctor pursed her lips. "Anything else?"

"I think we've reached an understanding now."

"Fine," she said smartly and turned and walked away.

I hated to see her look like that. She wasn't a bad lady, but folks who are so driven sometimes lose sight of common sense.

Tristan reached out for my hand.

I nodded to him then we headed down the hallway away from the doc's lab. Along the way, however, we came across Mister Iago who was headed in the doctor's direction. He kept his eyes low. Mister Iago tried to go around us, his eyes to the floor, but Tristan stepped in front of him,

"We are on lockdown. Where are you supposed to be?" Tristan asked him.

"I was just coming to see if the doctor needed help."

"Mister Iago, I will not see another device from your freak show in that lab. Do you understand me?" Tristan asked, his voice icy.

It wasn't like Tristan to be so riled up.

Mister Iago looked up at him from behind his thick glasses, his eyes wide. He looked just as surprised as I felt. "I'm just trying to help."

"Well, stop helping," Tristan said tersely then stepped aside. "And stay inside."

"Ye-yes, sir."

"I never did like him," Tristan whispered to me when we were out of earshot. "I used to pee on his van tires," he added with a chuckle.

"He isn't right, that's for sure…but all things considered," I said with a giggle, "you outta think about what *you* just said." It was still really hard getting used to the idea that Tristan had been my Puck.

Tristan grinned at me then led me down one of the little hallways that were all over the college. The college had strange, narrow passages behind the classrooms, near restrooms, all over. Most of them were marked staff/janitor only, but it had been a long winter and I was a curious woman. At the end of every one of those hallways was a locked door. Tristan led me to one of those doors then pulled out an old brass key and unlocked the door. Inside was a narrow stairwell. We went inside, Tristan locked the door behind us.

"And where, exactly, are we going?" I asked him.

"Somewhere with a good view," he replied.

We wound up the stairs, the scent of dust and old wood burning my nose, until we made our way to another locked door. Tristan unlocked it then led me inside.

It was clear to me at once that we were in the president's office.

The air inside the president's office was still. A large, fancy oak desk sat in the middle of the room. Oriental rugs covered the floor. The chairs all had expensive-looking leather upholstery. It was probably the most luxurious room I'd ever been in before. The walls were gray stones that had shimmering flecks that sparkled in the sunlight. Beams of lights streamed in through the window and reflected on the stained glass trim. Images of leaves, a massive old tree, and acorns decorated the window and cast green light on the floor. With a sigh, Tristan went to the window and looked out.

"I never stepped foot on a college campus until the day we got here," I said, picking up a crystal ball from the president's desk. It had bubbles inside. "Now I'm in the President's office. I thought they locked all the paintings and such in here."

"They are in the assistant's office outside," Tristan said, motioning absently to the big double doors on the other side of the room. The small door we came through didn't even look like a door from this side. It just looked like a panel in the wall.

"Secret passages?" I asked.

"It's a castle, after all," Tristan answered.

"See anything?" I asked, joining him at the window. I laced my hand in his then looked outside. We were at the very top of the building. From this angle we could see the horde that was moving slowly all around town. "They are everywhere," I whispered. I watched the undead move. Most of them moved real slowly, but others amongst them seem to move with purpose. It was strange.

"We're in danger," Tristan said quietly.

"When aren't we?"

Tristan shook his head. "Vampires, that rough crew, now this horde…it's no coincidence they've all stumbled across us."

"You mean someone is leading them here?"

"Yes."

"Who?"

"The dark forces in this world who mean to do you harm. I can't keep them out forever. They will find a way inside."

"And then what?"

Tristan turned and looked at me. "And then we run or we die."

"But run to where? Where are we going to go if they flush us out of here? We got old people here, and kids, and a whole lot of people who got soft sitting around playing Uno all winter. How in the world are we going to keep those folks safe?"

"We can't."

"Well, then I guess we better stop being so pessimistic then."

Tristan smiled down at me. "Is that what I am? Pessimistic?"

"I don't know," I replied. The sunlight made his hair shimmer with highlights of bronze and gold, his warm eyes shining with frustration and affection. His mixed expression made me laugh.

"What?" he asked then reached out to touch my cheek.

"We'll find a way. We have to, so we will. I don't plan to die any time soon."

"Neither do I."

"Too much livin' left to do," I said then leaned in to kiss him. His lips were so soft, his mouth hot. As soon as I planted my lips on him, it felt like I'd been set on fire. Tristan lifted me and carried me to the couch. He then pulled me onto his lap. He kissed my face and neck as he slid his hands under my shirt, stroking my back. He then pulled my shirt over my head.

He leaned back and looked at me. Taking my long braid into his hands, he pulled off the band at the end and gently unwound my wavy strawberry-blonde curls. I reached behind my back and unhooked my bra, tossing it to the side.

Tristan gazed at my breasts then began kissing me, touching me gently.

He slid his hands up my back and, breathing heavily, whispered in my ear. "Are you certain?"

"Never been more sure," I replied. Finally, I would have him. I stood and pulled off my jeans. Tristan chuckled when he saw my Super Girl panties. He didn't say a word, however, after I slid them off. Instead, he pulled off his pants, no underwear underneath, and guided me back onto his lap.

"I love you. I will do everything I can to keep you safe," he told me.

"All I want right now is you," I replied.

Then we fell into one another and were lost in the bliss of loving each other the way we wanted to for so long.

LAYLA

"How are you feeling?" I asked Jaime when he woke groggily. After returning to the college, I'd sent him and Kellimore both to bed. Elle, who said little but smoked what appeared to be the last of her cigarettes, had gone off to help Chase warn the others.

"Like someone is smacking my head with an anvil," Jaime replied.

"You want the doctor to check you out?" I asked. As much as I disliked Doctor Gustav, at the very least she could see if Jaime had a concussion.

"No, it's just a migraine. I think I spotted some heavy-duty painkillers in her lab, though. Would you mind?"

"Anything for you," I told him, kissing him on the forehead. I then headed out of the library and back to the doctor's lab. I wondered what Tristan had said to her when we got back. In the short while since we'd been there, I'd never seen him so angry. The doctor meant no harm. There was no way she could understand that we were being targeted by malevolent forces. I also knew Tristan was right. We were in danger and running on fool's errands helped no one.

The door to the lab was closed when I arrived. I knocked, but there was no answer.

I pushed the door open. The lamps were out, but the burners cast light and made shadows all around the room. I lifted a flashlight from the nearest table and clicked it on. I opened the medicine cabinet and found a bottle of prescription strength acetaminophen. I took out four tablets, intending to stop by Kellimore's room before I went back upstairs. Something told me he was hurting, despite his macho act.

I was about to turn to go when I felt that strange vibe from the other side of the room once more. She was there. I flicked an eye toward the lab door. Wherever the doctor went, perhaps off licking her wounds after what had been, no doubt, a horrendous scolding from Tristan, she wasn't going to be back soon.

Flashing my light, I headed toward the far side of the room and found the closet door unlocked.

Moving slowly, I opened the door.

The woman hissed. But when she saw it was me, she calmed and stepped back.

I set the flashlight on the counter nearby, facing its beam toward the ceiling. It cast long reflections of the woman and me against the wall. We stared at one another.

"I saw another one like you today, another undead who can hear me," I told her then, speaking out loud. "Can you understand me when I speak like this?"

"Yes," the reply came telepathically.

"You can't speak anymore?"

"No."

"There was an undead man. He helped me. I don't understand. You can still think, communicate, reason, but you're still eating the living. Why?"

"Famish. Nearly uncontrollable."

"Nearly?"

The woman didn't answer but came to the side of the cage and pointed once more at the closed door. *"Help me,"* she implored, and I felt the terrible desperation in her request.

"You must promise it's safe."

"Safe."

I looked at the woman once more, her white eyes imploring me. Something about the woman, the look on her face, was familiar. I couldn't place my finger on it.

Pulling my sword, I went to the closet. I could see very dim UV light from under the door. Moving slowly, I pushed the door open. Inside, I found a very small, dark closet. And inside that closet, sitting on a roller table, was an incubator. Within, a small baby, perhaps no more than one or two months old, lay on a stained white blanket. Its pale-colored arms fluttered with startle when I entered. I crossed the room and looked down at the tiny creature. It looked up at me. Its eyes were as white as the moon.

Gasping, I stepped back. My heart thundered in my chest. The tiny baby, unable to control its neck, kicked and let out a strange sounding whine. It wasn't a cry. It was a muted shrill of hunger.

I glanced around the dark room. The doctor had left her EEG equipment on a shelf nearby. She was planning to test the baby…the undead baby.

The undead woman rattled the bars. I searched her face. All at once, I realized where I knew her from. "You are the Stones' daughter," I said then.

"I am no one. Give me my baby."

Unlocking the brake on the roller, I pulled the incubator into the room where she was. There was no way for me to give the woman the child without opening her gate, but I rolled the incubator as close as I could then opened the lid. The tiny, toothless baby hissed at me. It hungered. I could feel its terrible need. But need for what? Blood? Mother's milk? Could the undead live and die as we did? Could an undead baby grow or was it stuck in its infantile form?

The undead woman kneeled then slipped her fingers through the bars, straining to reach her child. It was too much to bear. In my head, I heard her humming. She was trying to comfort the baby.

"Incredible, isn't it?" I heard Doctor Gustav say from behind me. "We discovered her and the child during the early stages of the outbreak. Right away I could see she was different from the rest. She was rabid in the beginning, much like the others, but I could see her thinking. She was intelligent in the way she tried to outmaneuver us, to protect her baby. These other creatures, they are stumbling around on instinct, only limitedly aware of their environment. But I could see she was different...as was her baby. When the disease first sets in, the infection inflames the brain. They all see red, are driven by the id. I've seen others like her, but haven't been able to study them. The distinctions between the undead, almost a year out, are starting to become clearer."

The woman rose and hissed at the doctor.

Doctor Gustav entered the room, closed the lid on the incubator, and pushed it back into the closet, closing the door behind her.

The undead woman went mad, banging and rattling the bars of her cage. I could hear her wailing agony in my head. It was too much to take.

"This is an abomination," I told the doctor.

"Yes," the doctor agreed.

"Not them. You."

The woman in the cage became still.

"Excuse me?"

"Tristan was right. You're a very dangerous woman. This isn't right. You said it yourself. She's different. Just because you can't communicate with her doesn't mean anything. This is wrong."

"Yes, she's different, but she's still little more than an animal. Just what should I do with her? Set her free? Throw her a baby shower?"

In the back of my head, I could hear Grandma Petrovich's voice: *slap her.* It took every ounce of my willpower to keep from doing just that.

"You will do nothing to her. Neither her nor her child."

"On what authority? You...so sanctimonious," she said, pointing her finger in my face. "Who do you think you are? Miss high and mighty. You arrived here just days ago and death follows you like a black cloud. We've lived in peace until you showed up. Now, everywhere we turn, trouble strikes."

"We are at war!"

"I believe I've found a way to stop this. Wouldn't that be better? I just need to test my theory, and then I'll prove it to all of you. You say we are in a war, but you are judging me for trying to fight it."

I stared at the doctor. There was no arguing with her. She could not know that the woman could actually communicate. She would never see anything other than the undead flesh.

"Don't touch her," I said then. "I'll discuss this matter with Tristan. Until then, leave them both alone. Her name is Elizabeth Stone. If I see you touch either of them again, you'll pay for it," I said then turned on my heel and headed back outside.

"They aren't alive, Layla," the doctor called after me. "Not anymore."

"Yes, they are. Just not the way you think," I answered, slamming the lab door behind me.

LAYLA

I rapped quietly on the door of the Athletic Coaches' office where Kellimore was staying. "Kellimore?" I called. "It's Layla."

"Yeah, come in."

The blinds on the window had been pulled down. The room was dim. On the walls were photos of soccer, football, basketball, and other sports teams. Trophies lined one wall, but they were covered in dust. I had similar trophies in my apartment in DC, relics from my matches. I imagined they'd all melted to nothing in the firebombing that had destroyed DC in the wake of the outbreak. Nearly everything I loved, both inside and outside Hamletville, was lost. Upstairs, just a handful of people I truly cared about remained. And once more, we were in danger.

Kellimore was lying on a cot. He sat up slowly.

"I brought you something for pain."

"I'll be all right," he replied.

"In a week," I said, then handed the pills to him.

He took the pills, swallowing them.

I glanced around the room. Spotting a water bottle, I handed it to him.

He took a sip then handed it back. "It's so quiet."

"Tristan has the place locked up. Your people are moving around everywhere, arming up, locking the place down.

"We'll be all right. This happened at the beginning too. They just pass us by. They don't even see us in here," Kellimore said, but I wasn't so sure.

"People say you're the one who saved everyone in town," I said, sitting down on the office chair.

Kellimore shrugged. "I love this town."

"When I was your age, I ran as fast as I could away from my hometown. But in the end, it saved me. Now all I wish is that I could go back."

"Na, you're good here with us. We needed another leader. People don't like Doctor Gustav much, Tristan weirds everyone out, and I'm just some dumb jock. You fit here."

"Hey, don't make fun of jocks," I said with a laugh as I put my hand on my sword.

Kellimore smiled then winced again.

"Get some rest. You need anything else?"

He shook his head.

I smiled at him then rose to go.

"Thanks...for earlier," he called.

"You owe me one," I replied then headed back into the hallway.

Kellimore was right. With all the blinds pulled and people hushed, the place was silent. I tried to head back upstairs but found several passages blocked. I finally found an open stairwell near the gymnasium, but at the top, I found the third floor cut off. I was beginning to sense that there was a flow to the placement of the gates. If anyone did get in, the gates would direct traffic...somewhere.

I tried to go down the hallway to the other stairwell, but it was closed as well. I turned to go back downstairs to look for another way back to the library, when a door opened. Vella stuck her head outside.

"I'm stuck," I told her, grinning abashedly.

She smiled at me. "Go there," she said, pointing to a classroom on the same side of the hall as her.

Nodding, I entered what looked like a nursing lab. There were diagrams of the human body on the walls and stacks of CPR dummies in the corner. I looked around but didn't see anything or anyone. After a moment, a door in the back opened.

"This way," Vella said, beckoning to me.

Thankful I'd brought the flashlight with me, I went to the back of the room and into what appeared to be a closet. Vella was standing inside that dark recess holding a flashlight.

"There is a panel in the back of the closet that opens to the other room. We all know the trick. All the closet doors work like this," she said then reached out for my hand and pulled me through. A moment later, I appeared in what looked like a faculty lounge. There were three cots there. Ariel was sitting on one of them, looking out the window from a crack in the blind. She glanced at me.

"Hi," she said, then went back to watching. "None of them are close yet."

Vella motioned for me to sit. "Have you seen Cricket?"

I shook my head. "Not since we got back. She went with Tristan."

Vella sighed heavily. "We saw Chase. He told us what happened. Is Jaime all right?"

"Banged up a bit," I replied. "I was just heading back with some meds for him."

"Then we won't keep you," she said and moved toward the door. It was then, however, that I saw she had a deck of tarot cards laid out on the table. I glanced at the cards. I was only mildly familiar with them. Grandma had never needed them. Her gift came from the other side, but it didn't take a fool to figure out that all the swords and death depicted in her spread wasn't a good thing.

"Do you know the tarot?" Vella asked me.

I shook my head. "But I know of it. My grandmother was a medium."

"Your grandmother?" From the way she said it, I could hear the question in her voice. *Your grandmother...not you too?*

I looked up at her. Vella's dark eyes were searching my face. "What do the cards say?" I asked.

"You don't want to know," Ariel answered for her.

"What do the spirits say?" Vella whispered to me.

"It's not the spirits who are talking to me," I replied softly.

"Then who?" Vella asked.

"You don't want to know," I replied.

She smiled, her lips pulling to one side, then nodded. "Check on your love. We will talk again soon," she said, leading me to the door.

I stepped outside to find that on this side of the gate, I could make my way back upstairs to the library.

"Thank you," I said.

Vella inclined her head then closed the door behind me.

She didn't have to tell me anything, but you didn't have to know the tarot well in order to figure out what was coming. The last card in Vella's spread was Death.

LAYLA

The library was eerily quiet. When I entered, Tom, Kiki, Will, and two men from the college I didn't know were sitting near the windows. They had drawn the blinds. Small holes had been cut so they could look through. They'd placed telescopes in the holes. The men were peering out.

"Still clear," Tom whispered.

Kiki shook her head. "We can't catch a break."

Will took her hand. "It'll be all right. They'll pass us by."

"Just like last time," one of the men said without looking back, but I noticed that both he and the other man were armed.

"Where are the others?" I asked.

"Frenchie put the girls down for a nap. She didn't want them looking outside. Ethel is...upset. Summer took her back to calm her. We haven't seen Buddie yet," Tom told me.

I nodded. "I'll be back, just let me take these painkillers to Jaime."

Tom looked puzzled. "But the doctor was already here."

"Sorry?"

"Doctor Gustav," Kiki said. "She brought Jaime some painkillers and antibiotics, I think."

"She was with Jaime? When?"

"You just missed her."

I nodded then headed back. The doctor must have been feeling guilty. It was her fault, after all, that this had happened to Jaime and Kellimore...and what had happened to Elle. I hadn't thought of grabbing antibiotics. Stupid on my part. Jaime's cut could get infected.

"Jaime?" I said, pushing the door opened slowly.

He was lying down. The room was dim. Sunlight cast shadows of the tree limbs across the blinds. Their shapes were gothic. They looked like long hands.

"Jaime?" I whispered.

He groaned lightly.

I kneeled down and put my hand on his shoulder.

"James?"

"Layla?" he whispered.

I set my hand on his forehead. Sure enough, he had a fever. I grabbed one of the water bottles and cursed myself for my stupidity. Why hadn't I thought to bring up the antibiotics? I needed to make sure Kellimore got some too.

"You okay, love?" I asked. "You're running a fever."

"My body is just fighting infection. The cut above my eye looked bad to Doctor Gustav. She gave me a shot, antibiotics and some painkillers. I should be feeling better by tonight. My head feels dizzy though," he said.

"Your stomach is empty. She probably doped you up a bit to cut the edge off the pain," I said. "Can you sit up so I can look at you?" I asked him.

He moved slowly, pushing himself up. He was terribly pale. "I think I might throw up," he said.

I reached for the waste can nearby, but Jaime waved it away and instead motioned for me to hand him the bottled water. He took a sip.

"Thank you," he whispered. "Layla...how is it out there? They didn't find us yet, did they?"

"No," I said, taking his hands in mine. They were burning.

"We need to be ready, just in case," Jaime told me groggily. "Why is it I'm always banged up whenever it's time to run?"

"You're just lucky, I guess. And we won't have to run. We're going to be fine." I leaned forward to look at the cut above Jaime's eye. It had been bandaged, but I could see that it was much more swollen than it had been.

"Layla…" Jaime said then. He reached out and touched my cheek. "My beautiful Layla."

I smiled at him, trying to hide my worry.

"I stopped when we went into town," Jaime said then started digging into his pocket. "I wanted…" he began, pulling something out, but then he paused and looked deeply at me. "I should have done this sooner. I want you to know how much I love you. I love you, Layla. I'm sorry this can't happen in the way you deserve. But I love you, and I want you to be my wife," he said then opened his hand.

In the center of his palm was a beautiful diamond engagement ring. The ring bore a massive diamond at the center with two emeralds on either side. The band was platinum. I stared at the ring then back at Jaime.

"Jaime? I…"

"We can't do anything like we used to, but I love you. And I will love you the rest of my life," he said, then took my hand. But then he paused. "You didn't say yes yet."

"Yes! Of course, yes," I replied. In the middle of all the madness, the inexplicable was happening. For how many years I had wanted to be Layla Campbell. I just never expected that it would be Jaime, not Ian, who would ask. Tears wet my cheeks and my heart fluttered with joy. There was a horde of zombies about to overwhelm us, but I was deeply in love.

"Now we just have to live," he said, sliding the ring onto my finger.

"We will," I replied, pulling Jaime into a tight hug, pressing him hard against me.

Jaime kissed my cheek and stroked my hair. "My ribs hurt," he said with a slight chuckle.

"I'm so sorry," I said with a laugh then helped him lie back down.

"God, this thing really knocked me out," Jaime said then, scratching his arm.

I pushed his sleeve back to see a swollen red mark where he'd been given the injection.

"My fiancé," he said, reaching up to touch my chin.

"I love you," I told him.

"I love you too," he replied. "I should have waited, but I was afraid Kellimore would mess up and tell you. Now... now I can barely keep my eyes open."

"He knew?"

Jaime nodded.

"I just left him. He didn't say a word."

"I like that boy."

"Me too," I said then leaned over and kissed Jaime on the forehead. "You've made me so happy," I whispered. "Get some rest. This menace will pass then we'll find some champagne to celebrate."

"Agreed," Jaime said with a whisper then closed his eyes. It seemed like only moments later he'd fallen to sleep, his breathing low and deep.

While my words to Jaime were optimistic, the feeling in my stomach wasn't. I rose and went back out into the library where the others still sat in silent watch.

I motioned to Will, Kiki, and Tom.

The look on their faces told me that they already knew what I was going to say. "What is it?" Will asked.

"Move quiet, but start packing up our stuff. Will, see if you can get some food and other supplies."

"Got it."

"You know where they keep the ammo?" I asked him.

He nodded. "First floor. In the Admissions office."

"All right. I'll head there. Kiki, can you keep an eye on Jaime? He's really hurting."

"Sure, Layla. Hey, nice rock," she said, eyeing the diamond.

She was right. It must have been at least two carats. During the apocalypse, everything was priceless. I smiled. "Thank you."

Tom and Will grinned at me.

"Keep a close watch on the door, and if Buddie comes back, don't let him leave," I told Tom who nodded. "I'll round up the ammo. Get everything ready in case we have to move fast, but let the others rest."

Tom nodded.

I glanced back at the room where Jaime was sleeping. With him so groggy, I prayed we wouldn't have to move anytime soon. "I'll be back," I whispered to the others then headed out the door.

I glanced down at the diamond. Fate had a really strange sense of humor.

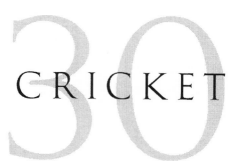

CRICKET

"There," I whispered, pointing. My heart slammed in my chest as the first of the zombies approached the gate. I stared out through the binoculars. The zombie at the front was male, a nasty looking piece of work, missing part of his face and one whole arm. How did something like that even happen? It was twilight. The sun had already set. The last light of day trimmed the horizon in a somber hazy gray. Behind the zombie, at least two dozen more undead approached the gate.

Tristan, Elle, Chase, and I had gone up to the bell tower at the very top of the college to take a look. Bill, one of the guys from town who had a good eye and a rifle with a scope, had been watching all afternoon. So far we'd been lucky. A handful of zombies had already meandered down Main Street and into the forest, not even following the road, just going back into the mountains. In the process, they'd missed us entirely. For the first time, however, some of the zombies had come to the college gate.

Tristan was silent as we watched, and I noticed he was looking all around the grounds, not just at the gate. Something on the west of the college suddenly caught his attention. Something moved through the forest toward the wall. Then, the new ferns on the base of our wall shook and a fox appeared inside the compound.

Tristan gasped and leaned forward.

"Fox," I said quietly. "We saw one in town this mornin'."

Tristan looked at me. "What?"

"Layla spotted it right before we got to the YMCA. It ran off."

Tristan looked at the fox then turned and glanced at the massive old tree at the back of the college.

"Tristan?"

For a split second, I thought I saw a blue light in the woods.

"Inside," Tristan whispered, motioning for Bill to come with us. "Now."

"Can they smell us or something?" Elle asked quietly.

"I don't know and I don't care," Chase answered as he opened the trap door of the bell tower, "but I know I'm headed to the armory."

"Quickly," Tristan said.

"Just because they're out there doesn't mean they can get in here," Bill said. But just as he finished the sentence, we all heard a strange sound. There was an odd grinding noise then the clatter of metal.

"What the...what the hell?" Elle said, amazed, and she leaned back against the rail of the bell tower.

We all moved back so we could see. There, standing on the inside of the fence, our side of the fence, was a woman with striking red hair. I'd never seen her before, and her clothes looked real...odd. She was wearing tanned leather pants, a fur coat, and had a bow strung across her back. With a loud clatter, she rolled away the interior door leaving only the outside gate. The undead grabbed at her, but she stealthily dodged their movements. She lifted the lock on the chain and studied it.

Tristan startled me then, shouting at her in a language I didn't understand. I didn't understand his words, but it was clear he was telling her to stop.

The woman turned, looked up at us, and then smiled slyly. She jabbed a dagger into the lock and turned it. The massive old padlock opened, and the woman slipped the chain off the gate, dropping it to the ground. She stepped back as the zombies pressed at the gate. Just before the group pushed through, light shimmered around the woman. In an instant, she turned into a small, red fox.

"Did you see that?" Chase asked in amazement. "Did anyone else see that?"

I looked up at Tristan.

"Let's go," he said, grabbing my hand.

We hustled down the stairs.

"I need to get to my family," Bill said, taking off down the hallway.

"I'll go to the armory," Chase said then turned, but Tristan grabbed his arm.

"No," Tristan said. "Elle, stay with us," he told her then turned back to Chase. "Go get Vella, Ariel, and Darius. Pack quickly and meet us at the south end of the building."

"Why?" I asked Tristan.

"Time to run."

LAYLA

I was stuffing ammo into a backpack when I heard a loud clatter from outside. I pushed aside the blind to see more than two dozen zombies push open the gate. And more than that, I saw a fox loping away.

"Time to go," a voice said from behind me.

I turned to see my grandma, and see through her, all at once. "Grandma?"

"Go, Layla. Quickly."

"Go where?"

"With the leshi. Go now. My Layla, I'm so sorry."

"Grandma?"

But my grandmother had already faded. I slung the backpack over my shoulder and headed down the hallway.

Everywhere I looked, the college survivors were running off to take cover.

"They broke through," the woman, Gwen, had told me. "What do we do?"

"Stay low and quiet. Stay behind closed doors. And if you have to, get ready to run," I replied.

She nodded then pushed a bundle at me. "Med kit," she said, then took off down the hall.

My heart was slamming in my chest. I needed to get the others out of this place. And I needed to find Tristan. But I sure as hell wasn't planning to leave these people behind.

At the end of the hallway, I heard a slamming on the outside door. Dim shadows pressed against the glass, and I heard the familiar groan of the undead. It was getting dark outside. The corridors, all shuttered, were dimly lit. Dammit.

I rushed down the hallway toward the Student Union. On the way, I passed a group of people rushing to the armory.

"We'll pick them off from the rooftop," one of the men was saying. "I've got my scope," he added.

"No, don't," I called to them, stopping.

The men paused and looked back at me.

"The noise will attract others."

The men frowned and looked at one another.

"Okay, let's just ammo up then...just in case," one of them said. "We need Kellimore. Where is that boy?"

"He's banged up," I told them.

"Don't worry about Kellimore. We can handle it," another man said then they turned and moved off.

I ran back to the stairs but paused. Kellimore would still be asleep. No doubt, no one had told him. I turned and headed back down the hallway toward Kellimore's room. When I got there, I knocked gently then pushed the door open.

"Kellimore?" I called.

I could see he was still resting. "Yeah?"

"It's Layla."

"Oh, I thought maybe it was the doc again. The last thing I need is a freaking shot," he said, sitting up, but then he looked at me, reading the expression on my face. "What is it?"

"They've breeched the wall."

"What?" he asked, sitting up. "How in the hell did that happen?"

"I don't know how, but I saw them come in. Listen," I said. From outside, you could hear the groans.

"They running the lockdown procedure? They got the gates in place?" Kellimore asked me.

"Tristan was on it. I see gates up. A group just headed off to the armory."

"Why?" he asked, standing. "Wait, they aren't going to go outside, are they?"

My stomach dropped. "I...I don't know. I thought they were just gearing up in case they broke in."

But a moment later, we heard a gate rattle followed by the screech of the front double doors.

"Fuck!" Kellimore said as he started pulling on his boots. "Those idiots. They're going to let those bastards in by mistake."

I knew he was right. Lending Kellimore a hand, I helped him stand then we both ran toward the noise. Sure enough, five men armed with baseball bats and knives had headed outside.

"Oh, my God, they're going to be slaughtered," I said. "We need to help them." I realized then that Kellimore was leaning heavily against the wall.

To my great relief, just then Buddie turned the corner. "Did you see that?" he asked me. "A group went out there. They're trying to close the gate. Layla..."

"I know," I said, then pulled off my pack and set it down. I unsheathed my shashka and looked at Buddie who nodded.

"Guard the door," I told Kellimore. "If we get overrun, lock the place up," I said.

"I can help," he protested.

"Yes, by staying inside and keeping the place locked up. You need to rest."

Before Kellimore could protest, I turned to Buddie. "Let's go," I said then we headed outside.

There were six men in a fray with about two dozen undead. They were barely holding their own. I glanced toward the gate. A handful more zombies had meandered inside.

"The gate," Buddie said, as if he read my mind.

Nodding, Buddie and I ran across the lawn toward the front entrance. Buddie paused to launch a few arrows at the undead nearest us. As near as I could tell, they were all rotting undead. I moved quickly, sliding my blade through an undead man's head as we moved. He fell on the ground. Again, an undead woman lunged at me, but I decapitated her before she could reach me. Blood splatted on my jeans. It was dark. The moon was shining overhead, offering us just enough light to see. Buddie and I rushed quickly to the gate.

When we looked outside, however, we were shocked. Hundreds of undead were coming down the street toward the college. Near the front, I saw the undead man from the YMCA who'd helped me. His purposeful movements set him apart from the others. He stopped when he saw Buddie and me.

"Run," his voice came to me. *"Run."*

"Quickly," I told Buddie.

Buddie and I slapped the gate shut, pushing down the u-shaped lock, then, together, we slid the second door into place, but not before the massive horde reached the gate.

Their stench arrived before they did. The smell of meat and decay, a sharp scent of rot assailed my nose. They groaned in hunger. Before we could get the gate closed, their long arms reached through the bars.

"Push," Buddie said.

We pushed hard, sliding the rolling metal gate in place, pressing against the undead limbs sticking through the gate. From the corner or my eye, however, I spotted movement. Out of the darkness, an undead man stumbled toward Buddie.

"Buddie," I screamed.

He pulled his knife and turned, but it was too late. The undead man took a huge bite out of Buddie's neck. He fell to the ground, writhing in pain, but managed to stab the undead man through the eye. He let go of the knife then stood again.

Breathless, I stood staring at my friend. Grief threatened to overwhelm me. "Buddie?"

From the other side of the gate, the undead groaned and pushed.

"Let's finish the job," he said, then pushed the rolling gate once more.

Together, Buddie and I rolled the secondary gate into place and locked it. Buddie then collapsed against the gate, blood dripping from his neck down his chest. I knelt on the ground beside him. I ripped the bottom of my T-shirt off and moved to stop the bloodletting.

"No, don't touch it. You could get sick too. Layla," he said, taking my hand. "Go," he said then winced. "Get our people out of here. Take them home. This world is done anyway. At least let them die in Hamletville," he said then shifted in pain. "I'll stay here," he said, pulling his gun from its holster. "I can still watch the gate...do what I can."

"I can't just leave you here," I said, tears streaming down my cheeks. "This can't be happening."

"It's already happened," he said with a groan. "Go, Layla. Please. This gate won't hold forever, not with a horde that size."

"I..." but I didn't know what to say.

"If you see me, shoot me...if I don't get to it first."

I noticed he was beginning to turn very pale.

"Buddie," I whispered.

"Get them out of here," he said. "Hurry."

My eyes held his for a moment longer then I turned and ran back toward the college. The group of rash men had apparently run off, the undead following. One of the men lay on the ground. I bent to check him. He was dead. Reluctantly, I stabbed him through the eye, not wanting him to reanimate.

I turned and headed back up the stairs to the door where I'd left Kellimore, but was met with a surprise. The door was locked and Kellimore was gone. I pressed my face against the glass. My backpack was gone too. Dammit.

"Enemies without…and enemies within," a female voice called from behind me.

I turned to look. In the gathering darkness, I saw the shape of the fox woman standing among the trees. Her eyes glimmered like an animal's in the dark of night.

"I know what you are now," I told her.

From the yard below, I heard zombies pounding on the gate and the massive chorus of groaning voices.

"Then you know there is no use in running. Your time…is over. We will take our earth back."

"Seems like you have some unexpected company," I replied, motioning toward the undead.

"True. A complication we didn't foresee, but not one with much longevity. In a year, all that will be left is their bones."

She didn't know. The kitsune had not yet realized that not all the undead were so…dead.

From across the lawn, I heard Buddie's voice rise as he shouted at someone. Then, there was a gunshot, then another, which was followed by a muffled yell. A moment later, I heard the gate screech as it was rolled back out of place.

"Like chickens in a pen. Where will you hide now?"

I pulled my sword and rushed the woman who dodged out of the way. She was incredibly fast. She grinned at me.

I lunged at her again. This time, the tip of my blade caught her hair and the length of her braid fell to the ground. She looked at it, then at me, then snarled. And with a flash of yellow light, she transformed into a fox and ran off into the darkness. As she did so, she barked loudly. And from the darkness of night, I heard several other barks in reply.

There was a massive crash as the heavy metal gate fell to the ground.

They were inside.

Turning, I ran down the path toward the side entrance of the college, praying someone would see me. Who in the hell had locked that door! Where had Kellimore gone?

I reached the door outside the doctor's wing. Through the closed door, I could see light in the doctor's lab and someone moving around. Knowing noise would attract the undead, but also knowing I didn't have a choice, I pounded on the door. "Hey! Someone! Let me in!"

The shadow paused. "Here! I'm outside," I called desperately, fully aware I was going to need to run if someone didn't come.

A moment later, someone stepped into the hallway and pushed the accordion gate open. A little man with large glasses, and even larger eyes, stared at me from the other side of the door. Mister Iago, the freak show man, stood looking at me.

"I tried to shut the gate but got locked out. They've breached the walls. Please, let me in," I said.

The man stared at me. My skin rose in goosebumps when I realized he was considering.

"Please," I said softly.

Mister Iago frowned then unlocked the door.

I slid inside, pulling the door closed behind me. Mister Iago and I headed back down the hallway where he slid the accordion door closed, locking it in place.

"Thank you," I said, then looked into the lab. "The doctor?"

"She's not there," he told me. "I was just gathering my things," he said, picking up a large wooden box. "Good luck, ma'am," he added and headed back down the hallway into the darkness.

I stared into the doctor's lab, a dim light shining therein, then turned away. I needed to get to Jaime. I raced down the hallway, following the path I'd taken earlier that day, to the room where I'd met Vella. Snapping on my flashlight, I crossed the nursing lab then slid the panel open to enter the room where I'd met Vella and Ariel earlier that day. They were gone, and so were all of their things. Had they left? Had Tristan and their group abandoned us?

From outside, I heard the bark of a fox once more followed by the sound of breaking glass. Moments later, I heard screaming downstairs. The kitsune were letting the undead inside. I ran upstairs and down the hallway to the library. Inside, it was totally dark. All the lights were out, and I didn't hear anyone.

"Tom?" I called. "Jaime?"

For a moment, I was met by silence then I heard a voice. "Layla?" It was Summer.

"I'm here," I said. "We need to go. Where is everyone?"

"Here," Tom said, clicking on a flashlight.

The Hamletville group emerged from a study room.

"Where is Buddie?" Ethel asked.

I shook my head.

Ethel inhaled a deep, shuddering breath.

"We need to be strong," I said. "The college is overrun. We need to get out. There is a way out of the back of this compound. We'll need to climb, but we can get out if we move fast and stay together," I said. "There are some vehicles in town. We can take those and drive out of here."

"But they were locked up," Will said.

"When did that ever stop us before?" I replied.

"Did you get the ammo?" Will asked.

I shook my head, still uncertain what had happened to my pack. I hoped wherever Kellimore was, he had it with him.

"Where's Jaime?" I asked.

"Sick," Summer said. "We didn't dare move him."

I nodded. "We've got to go. Frenchie, you and the girls ready?"

"We're ready," Kira said.

I looked at Tom and Will who nodded, understanding. Frenchie would need their help.

"I'll get Jaime," I said then ran back to our room.

I pushed open the door to find Jaime still lying on the makeshift bed. "Time to go," I told him. "Fever or no, we're running for our lives again."

"Layla," Jaime said weakly. "Layla, my whole body hurts."

I touched his forehead. He was burning with fever. Dammit.

"Doesn't matter. It will hurt a lot more if zombies eat you," I said then pulled him to his feet. He was soaked in sweat. "Hey, you already had the flu this year," I told him. "This isn't the best time for a cry for attention," I said jokingly.

Jaime gave a muffled laugh. "It might be sepsis. My head feels so weird. My heart is beating so loudly."

How in the hell was I going to keep Jaime safe? He could barely walk. Using all my strength, I held onto Jaime and led him out to the main room.

"Oh, Jaime," Ethel said. "You look horrible."

"Infection," he replied. "And an ass-kicking. I'll be okay."

"Let's go," I said, then led them into the darkened hallway. From the first floor, we heard screaming and gunshots.

"That's not good," Tom whispered.

"Mommy, I'm scared," Susan said.

Where in the hell was Tristan? How could he just leave us like this? But then my brain switched gears. What if Tristan wasn't what he said he was after all? What if he was just another one of them? But that couldn't be. My grandmother had said to find the leshi. That was, of course, if I hadn't imagined it.

We moved down the darkened hallway to the stairwell. I motioned for Tom to click off his flashlight. We stood in complete darkness. It was clear, at least for the moment. I motioned for them to follow me downstairs.

"Can you make it?" I whispered to Jaime.

He didn't seem to hear me and nearly stumbled on the steps.

I took Jaime from one side, Will taking him from the other, and we wove down the stairs. From the other end of the long building, on the second floor, we heard screams and the sound of gunfire.

I motioned for the others to cross the hall into the faculty lounge.

We were just crossing the hallway when the first group of zombies came up the stairs. The gate closing off the second floor shook as they ran into it, rattling and shaking the gate.

"This way," I called, leading them into the faculty lounge and heading toward the back closet. I had just pushed the closet open when I heard the gate in the hallway come crashing down.

"Shit!" Kiki called from the back.

"Go," I said, motioning for Will to lead Jaime through. Tom followed behind with Kira and Susan in tow.

Ethel and Summer were just ducking through when the first of the undead staggered into the room. There were maybe a dozen of them, their mouths wet with fresh blood.

Will and I both pulled out our guns and started firing.

"We're asking for company," Kiki warned.

"Go, go," I said to them. They slid through the panel to the other side. Coming in last behind them, I slid the closet door shut. We were in the nursing lab. I could hear the zombies on the other side of the closet door knocking against the wall.

"Come on," Will said as he and Jaime pushed forward and back out into the hallway. We exited the room. When the zombies on the other side of the gate saw us, they started pushing on the gate.

"We need to get out of the building. Head down to the first floor and out the side door. It may be grim," I said, then moved forward. I stopped at the stairwell and listened. Nothing. As usual, the doctor's end of the hallway was silent. "Let's go," I said, then we moved quickly down the stairs. The hallway was completely dark. We could hear gunshots from the other side of the building but nothing on this end.

"We need to help those people," Ethel said.

"We will, but first I need to get you all to safety," I said.

Moving quietly, I passed the doctor's lab. A single lamp burned inside.

"Layla," Will whispered. "Grab some meds for Jaime," he said, jerking his chin toward the lab as he heaved Jaime up. "He's almost out."

"I got the gate," Kiki said as she slowly unlocked the accordion door.

Moving quickly, I stepped into the lab and opened the medicine cabinet. I grabbed several packs of antibiotics and stuffed them into my pocket. When I turned to go back, however, I saw the flu vaccine Cricket had found sitting exposed on the table. The lamp light illuminated a number of vials sitting beside it, and some fresh syringes. A chill washed over me.

"Hey, who are you?" I heard Kiki ask from the hallway followed by the sound of the outside door opening.

"Get back," Tom yelled.

Summer screamed.

I turned to see all of them rush into the lab, a horde of zombies flowing in behind them.

"Jesus Christ, some woman just let them inside," Kiki yelled as she pulled her gun and started firing.

"Mommy," Susan screamed as she clung to Tom.

The undead moved quickly, rushing into the room after them.

Ethel tripped and fell.

Summer stopped to pick her up.

As if in slow motion, I saw the zombies overwhelm them. Summer tried to pull the knife I had given her, but it was too late. She screeched as they fell on her, shoving her to the ground, taking massive bites out of her back. Ethel tried to fight, pushing the undead off Summer. But there was nothing she could do. She howled in torment but then an undead man grabbed her and bit into her throat, silencing her cries.

Kira screamed.

Frenchie, clutching her daughter, looked wild-eyed at me. "Layla!"

"Here," I yelled, racing across the room to the closet where Doctor Gustav had penned up the creature that had once been Elizabeth Stone.

Will pushed Jaime toward Tom and he and Kiki stood shooting as we fell back.

I opened the door to find the undead woman still inside, still locked in the cage. Her eyes met mine. I motioned Frenchie and girls in. Kira shrieked when she saw the woman.

"Tom, Jaime," I called, and reached out to take Jaime who fell heavily against me. "Jaime?" I whispered.

"Layla," he said, then fell to the ground.

Kiki and Will were falling back, but I watched in horror as Kiki's gun jammed. She paused just for a moment, but it was a moment too long. An undead woman grabbed her.

"Kiki," Will yelled, firing, but it was too late.

Kiki went down with a scream.

Several of the undead, momentarily preoccupied by what was left of our friends, halted their pursuit.

"Dammit, Will, come on," I yelled. I stepped out, pulling him into the room, then slammed the door shut behind us.

"Mommy," Kira said. "Mommy! Layla! Look!"

The others turned then and saw the undead woman. Will pulled his knife. The undead woman hissed at him and stepped back.

"No," I said, stopping Will's arm. "No."

"No?"

"What do we do now?" Tom whispered.

I bent low to check on Jaime. He was very nearly unconscious. "Jaime? James?"

"Layla," he whispered.

Tom and I propped him up against the wall.

Kira and Susan where whimpering quietly, their faces pressed into Frenchie's legs. The room was dim, but there were long shadows cast by the UV light from under the door to the interior closet.

"Is there another way out of here?" I asked the undead woman.

She looked at me but didn't reply.

"Elizabeth," I said sharply to her. "Is there another way out of here?"

"Layla, what in the hell are you doing?" Will whispered, aghast.

"Give me my baby," came the reply.

I opened the door to the closet. The incubator was still inside. Gently, I rolled it into the room.

"Is that…" Tom said, looking down at the baby.

"Her baby," I said. I opened the lid on the incubator.

The undead slammed against the closet door. There were so many of them, too many.

"Is there another way out of here?" I asked the undead woman again.

"A panel in the wall. In there," she said, motioning to the closet.

I went into the other room and felt along the wall. Sure enough, there was an unseen panel. I clicked the lock and the panel slid open. I looked inside. It was narrow, but quiet. It smelled like the basement in the Hamletville library.

"Where does it lead?" I asked her, coming back.

"I don't know."

"Into the passage," I told my shell-shocked group. "There. We'll find our way out."

"Layla, what the hell is going on?" Frenchie asked me.

"I can hear her," I replied.

"How?" Frenchie asked.

I tapped my head with one finger. "Not all of them...just some. Go," I said then.

Without another word, Tom lifted Jaime from the ground and led him into the hallway. "Tight fit, buddy," Tom told Jaime. "Work with me here, old friend."

Jaime grunted absently in reply.

Frenchie took the girls and followed behind them.

"Layla?" Will called as he ducked into the wall.

"Coming," I replied, then lifted my sword and dropped it on the chain penning Elizabeth in. It fell to the ground. I reached out and opened the gate. Then, remembering, I dug into my pocket. There I found the photo I'd taken from the Stone's house. With a shaking hand, I handed it to the undead woman.

"I'm sorry this happened to you."

The undead woman took the photo, looked at it, and then set it aside. Moving carefully, gently supporting the undead baby's neck, she lifted her child and pressed it against her. She squeezed her eyes shut tight.

"Thank you."

"Layla?" Will called.

From the room outside, however, I was startled by the sound of gunfire. Maybe it was Tristan.

"Who is in here?" I heard a voice call.

It was Doctor Gustav.

"Layla, let's just go," Will said harshly.

There was more gunfire from the outer room.

The undead woman looked stunned. Her white eyes popped open. She gently set her baby down, then her eyes flashed toward the door.

"Get back," I heard Doctor Gustav say, followed by another gunshot. There was a commotion, and I heard the sound of clattering equipment and grunting.

"Layla," Frenchie called from the alcove.

The undead woman bent over her child, kissed it on the forehead, and then looked up at me.

"*Go,*" she said then opened the door. Moving faster than I had imagined possible, the woman slipped out the door. Seconds later, I heard Doctor Gustav scream. From the crack in the door, I saw the mangled remains of Kiki on the floor and beside it, I saw that the undead woman had pushed Doctor Gustav down and was taking massive bites from her neck, splashes of scarlet colored blood spraying everywhere.

Doctor Gustav screamed a gurgling sound, her feet thrashing wildly, then she fell silent.

I stepped into the corridor and slid the panel closed behind me.

32 CRICKET

"We can't leave those people behind," Elle said indignantly as Tristan waved us all down a back service stairwell.

I saw a frustrated look cross Tristan's face. "We won't," he said then paused, looking from Vella to me. "Let me take you somewhere safe, then I'll come back for the others. And I need to find Layla."

"Why don't we get everyone rounded up first?" I said to him. While I knew Tristan was looking out for Vella and me, it didn't feel right. I couldn't just leave everyone else behind to save my own hide.

"Cricket," he said. "Please."

"Na, man, not like this. Let's save who we can. If you got a plan to run, let's let everyone else in on it," Chase told him.

"Exactly," Elle echoed.

Frustrated, Tristan sighed, and I heard him grumble "humans" under his breath. "Quietly," he told us. "And keep your eyes open. We have other enemies lurking, not just the undead."

"What was she?" Elle whispered.

"Your reaper," he replied, then motioned for us to follow.

A tremor went down my body. Reaper. What a word. I clicked on my Maglite, and followed Tristan down the stairs. The space was very narrow and dusty. From the other side of the walls, we could hear screaming and gunfire. My hands were shaking. How in the world were we going to run in the dark? Tristan was right, there were all sorts of things bumping around in our world now. Where could we go? *Daddy? Watch over us, Daddy.*

The stairwell led to the first floor. When we reached the bottom, we found another locked door. Tristan pulled out his keys. I shined a light on the lock. On the other side of the wall, we heard a scream.

"Was that Gwen?" Ariel whispered.

"The building is breeched," Tristan whispered. "We'll exit on the south lawn, see if we can find anyone in the west wing, then make for the south wall."

The door popped open. Tristan led us to a set of spiral stairs toward the basement. I wasn't keen on being down there. Before we'd come to the college, they'd used the basement as a place to wrangle all the undead then pick them off through windows all along the top of the basement. Moving slowly, Tristan pushed the door open and stepped out.

It was eerily silent and the smell of death hung in the air.

"This way," Tristan whispered, leading us along the south wall. Moving quietly, he opened the doors to what looked like a root cellar. Inside, however, I saw lawn mowers, weed eaters, and all kinds of equipment. We pushed past the equipment to the outside wall. The door leading away from the maintenance shed was locked. Tristan turned, grabbed an axe from the wall, and motioned for us to stand back. With a few heaves, he chopped the chain, the lock falling to the ground.

"This might come in handy," Darius said, pulling a hand-held sickle from the walls. I looked back at him. We were all wearing our packs, and all of us — even Ariel — were carrying weapons. Lord knows she was a good shot. Kellimore spent all winter — and used up most of the paint ball pellets — teaching her how to shoot.

I checked my pistol again. It was loaded, the safety off. It felt weird to have my machete strapped around me again. I held onto my wrench.

"Ready?" I whispered to Vella.

She shook her head. "No matter what, do what Tristan tells you," she whispered to me.

"What...what do you mean?"

Vella frowned. In the dim shadow of the reflected flashlight, I could see worry written all over her face. "As I said."

"Let's go," Tristan whispered, pushing hard against the door, which was reluctant to open. The tall grass outside didn't want to budge. Tristan pushed hard, opening the door wide enough so we all could shimmy outside.

It was dark. It took a minute for my eyes to adjust, but there was enough moon to cast a glow and the sky was mostly clear. Most of the chaos we heard was happening inside the building. On the campus green, it was clear. We kept low and followed the south wall down the side of the building. I glanced around. In the distance, I spotted the massive old tree. I was pretty sure that I knew where Tristan was taking us. But in case I'd had any doubts, I saw, for just a moment, blue light flicker around the branches.

I grabbed Vella's arm. "You see that?" I whispered.

"Yes," she replied, her voice firm.

Tristan turned then, motioning for us to follow him across the lawn to the west entrance of the building. The door, which had been locked, was broken and wagging wide open. Motioning for us to stay back, Tristan clicked off his flashlight and slowly went up the steps. We watched as he listened, but then his posture changed and I heard the groan of the undead.

Tristan stepped back down the stairs as at least six of the undead came lumbering out the door. Moving fast, Chase and I ran up on them. I gripped my wrench tight and smashed a rotted, undead woman in the side of the head. Goo and a mess of rotted teeth splashed across my cheek as I turned just in time to avoid having it go into my mouth. Before I even had a chance to wipe the goop away, another undead woman came up on me, but Darius moved in with his sickle and lopped off her head which I then stabbed with my machete. I turned in time to see that Chase and Tristan had taken down the others. Vella stood with her small hunting knife ready, but she hadn't entered the fray.

We all waited then, looking at the dark hallway. There was no sound, no sign of life or anything else.

"We gotta check the classrooms," I said. "We need to look inside."

Tristan seemed reluctant so Chase took the lead. He clicked on his flashlight and scanned the hallway. It was then that I could see bodies lying in the hall. I saw Gwen and her family, including her boys. They had been ripped up almost beyond recognition.

I moved past Tristan who stood standing, looking inside. He gently took my arm. "Cricket, we need to go."

"Not yet," I replied and moved past him.

Darius and Ariel entered behind me. I saw Vella and Tristan exchange low but sharp words, and a minute later they both entered.

Chase and I stood over the bodies of Gwen and her family. I nodded to him, and we both bent low, stabbing them through the skull. There wasn't much left of them, but I didn't want them to rise. It was too horrible to think of.

We moved carefully down the hallway, the sound of broken glass crackling under our feet. His shotgun drawn, Chase pushed open a classroom door with the barrel. I flashed my flashlight inside, hoping no one could see how bad my hands were shaking. The room was empty.

"Closet?"

"Anyone alive?" Chase called. "Come out."

There was nothing.

We moved on to the next room and then the next. Every room was empty, or in each room, we found nothing but mostly-eaten corpses. The gate at a junction in the hallway had been pushed over, ripped from the wall. Moving slowly, the others followed behind Chase and me. I was startled when I saw something move. The beam of my flashlight bounced off someone's glasses.

"Mister Iago?" I called, seeing the little man scurry down the hallway toting a heavy box along with him.

"Run, Cricket. They're coming," he said as he rushed toward me.

A moment later, a group of five or six zombies turned into the hallway after him. At the same time, my ears picked up the sound of shooting outside the building. Then I heard yelling. I raised my pistol to shoot the zombies coming toward me when more than a dozen more turned the corner.

"Cricket, Chase," Tristan called. "Let's go!"

I looked at Chase.

"Graveyard. We're too late," Chase said and we turned and ran toward the exit.

I could hear Mister Iago's box jangling as he struggled to keep up.

"Mister Iago, leave that box," I yelled to him.

"I...I can't. My show..."

The carnival. Dammit. I stopped, turned, and sprinted back to him.

"Cricket, come on," Chase called.

Slipping my gun into the back of my pants, I grabbed the box from Mister Iago's hand, holding tight to my pipe wrench with the other, and took off down the hallway. Damned thing was heavy, but I knew...I understood.

We raced out of the hallway, Darius and Ariel taking aim at the undead following behind us. We made it in time. In time to walk into a firefight.

LAYLA

Sliding past the others, I moved to the front, clicked on my flashlight, and headed down the narrow passage.

"That undead woman, you heard her?" Tom asked me.

"Yes," I replied, my hands shaking. Elizabeth Stone was undead, that was certain. And she could communicate with me telepathically, that was also certain. She loved her child, that was also true. But in the end, she had eaten Doctor Gustav alive just like the other undead would have done. I understood her rage, but one thing was still very clear. Just because some of the undead were sentient, it didn't mean they were still us. Mankind had not died. We had transformed into a darker version of ourselves. On sun island, the fox woman had said that mankind had finally gone wendigo. She was right. Some corpses walked, and they were every bit the zombies we'd seen in the movies, but mankind…mankind was now something very different. We had become the violent shadow self that lurks inside us all.

"How?" Tom asked.

"Like Grandma used to hear the spirits, I suppose. They're dead, after all, just not in spirit form."

I glanced back at Jaime who was shuffling along with Tom's guidance. "Jaime, you okay? Can you make it?"

"Yeah," came an exhausted reply.

I looked up at Tom who was wearing a worried expression. Dammit.

We wove down the dusty hallway until it reached what appeared to be a dead end. I listened for a moment. It was quiet on the other side of the wall. I held my flashlight in my teeth then felt all along the wall. If what I knew about castles was correct, I could find a lock mechanism…there.

With a click, the door loosened and I pushed the panel slowly aside. I was surprised to find that it opened into a strange little alcove with a seat. I clicked off the flashlight and tried to look.

"A confessional," Tom whispered. "We must be in the chapel."

I had seen confessionals in churches before, but had never been inside one. I stepped inside the small space, a dark wooden room with a seat that had a red velvet cushion. There was a woven screen between this side of the confessional and the other. A similar screen looked outside. I gazed out. It was dark, but moonlight shimmered through the windows high above. It cast a strange blue light on the chapel. All along the walls, the white-marble saints were shadowed in a bluish hue.

I pushed the door to the confessional open and stepped out, motioning for the others to wait. There were glass doors at the other end of the room that led back into the college. In the distance, I heard gunshots. We needed another way out. There was a side door. I then remembered that I'd seen an amphitheater nestled along the back wall of the college. Outdoor mass? I eyed the door. It was locked with a simple slide bar.

"This way," I said.

Holding my sword in front of me and moving slowly past the pews, I led the others to the door. With a push, I undid the lock and opened the door. I looked around outside. It was quiet.

"We'll head to the south wall," I said. If I had guessed right, I knew where Tristan would go. Now I just needed to figure out how I was going to get Jaime up the tree and over the wall. The girls would be okay. I had worried about getting Ethel over the wall. One of these days, when I had a minute to feel, I worried my mind would collapse in on me. I had known Summer and Ethel all my life. Just like that, they were gone. At the least, Kira and Susan were still alive. I'd made good on that promise.

We slipped out of the chapel and into the night. Moving low and slow, we crossed the lawn to the wall. I breathed a sigh of relief.

"Lights off, eyes open," I whispered, and we made our way toward the tree. For a moment, I swore I saw blue light shimmer around the base of the old oak. Seemed like my hunch was right. My relief, however, was short-lived. A moment later, from across the lawn, I heard screaming, breaking glass, and a barrage of gunfire. I recognized the sound of my automatic.

Startled, we stopped and stared as the glass door behind the union shattered in a thousand pieces as Kellimore and a group rushed outside. There must have been at least fifty undead following behind them.

They stopped and shot at the oncoming horde. A moment later, I heard gunfire coming from the west end of the college and saw Cricket and Chase firing at the undead.

"Kellimore! South lawn," Cricket yelled. She was leading them to the same place we were headed. My fingers tingled and everything inside me wanted to go and help them, but I looked back at Jaime, who was wilting, and Kira and Susan who were clinging to Frenchie and Will for dear life. No. I had my own responsibilities. And I had already failed miserably.

I turned to Tom. "Go, go, let's go."

We took off at a run down the lawn toward the massive old tree.

"Look mommy, fire flies," Kira said as we headed toward the tree.

"Is that tree glowing?" Frenchie asked breathlessly.

Tom and Jaime were falling behind as Tom struggled to keep Jaime on his feet.

I looked at the tree. Kira was right. It was glowing. Tristan's people were trying to save us.

"There's Layla," I heard Vella call.

I looked back just in time to see Vella and Ariel racing across the lawn toward us, the others falling in behind them. Tristan cast a glance back at me, a whisper of a smile crossing his face, then he turned and shot into the undead.

Soon, we reached the base of the tree.

"Will, you first. Up and over. Make sure it's clear," I said, taking Susan from his arms.

Will moved fast. When he got a clear look, he flashed around his flashlight.

"Clear," he called.

"Up you go. Hold on tight and go slow toward Will," I told Kira.

Will moved across the branches toward her and I saw him gently guide the little girl.

"Piggy back," he told her, and when he was sure she was safe, he dropped.

"Just like your sister," I told Susan, first helping Frenchie up on the branch then handing Susan up toward her.

"Layla," Tom called.

I looked over my shoulder to see that Jaime had fallen to the ground.

"Up you go," I told Susan. "Get on Mom just like your sister did."

"Layla," Frenchie's voice came in a rattle.

"One foot at a time and hold on tight," I told her then ran to Jaime.

"He groaned then just dropped," Tom said then pulled his gun, standing protectively over Jaime and me.

"Jaime?" I whispered, kneeling down beside him. I slid my shashka into its scabbard. Jaime had crumbled to his side. I set my hand on his head, expecting to find he was burning with fever, but instead, he was deathly cold. "Jaime?" I said again, rolling him onto his back. I took a startled breath when I saw him looking glassy-eyed up at the sky, the moon reflecting in his eyes.

Vella dropped onto her knees beside me and pick up Jaime's hand, feeling for a pulse.

"He got an infection. It might be toxic shock. The doctor gave him something, but I don't think it's working. Jaime?" I called, but he didn't answer.

Startling me, Tom started shooting.

"Vella! Go," Tristan yelled at her as he rushed across the lawn toward us. "Up and over, up and over! Go now!"

Vella set her hand on my shoulder, and shook me just a little. I met her dark eyes.

"Whatever the doctor gave him…it's working. Time to say good-bye," she told me.

"What?"

"Vella," Tristan yelled.

I looked up to see that Tristan, Cricket, and Chase had nearly reached us. Elle, Ariel, Darius, and Mister Iago, followed behind. Thirty feet behind them, Kellimore and the others ran while fighting off a swarm of zombies. The young football star, outpacing the other college survivors even though he was hurt, looked like he might make it. The other college survivors fell screaming.

"James, get up now," I told him, then tried to pull Jaime to his feet. He wouldn't move.

"Layla, he's gone," Vella told me.

"What? No." I looked down at Jaime. "Jaime. Get up. Jaime. Do you hear me?"

He stared glassy-eyed at the moon, but after a moment, I realized what I was looking at. It wasn't the moon reflected in his eyes. His eyes had gone pale-white.

"Go," I heard Tristan tell the others. "Go, Cricket."

"What about — "

"I've got this."

"I'm sorry," Vella said, touching me gently on the shoulder. She rose, motioned for Tom to follow her, then they both left.

"Time to go," Tristan told me.

I looked up at him. "What…he wasn't bitten. I don't understand what happened."

"Yes, you do," Tristan said, giving me his hand to help me up.

I stood staring down at Jaime. The doctor had said she was certain she knew the cause, and she could prove it. I gazed at the man I loved. She'd proven it. She'd infected Jaime with the contaminant. She might have found the cure, but whatever it was, whatever she found, it was no good to me now. And I…I was the one who'd released her killer.

"Go, go, go," Kellimore shouted as he raced toward us.

I glanced at him. Kellimore was the only living person still moving toward us. A massive horde of undead followed him, but the others had not survived.

I looked down at Jaime. "I love you," I told him, feeling like my heart was shattering in half. How had this happened? His soft curls framed his pale face. He looked so peaceful lying there in the grass, staring up at the moon. "Jaime?" My knees went soft. I could barely stand.

"Come, Layla," Tristan said. He turned and pulled himself up into the tree and started moving across the branches. I pulled my gun and aimed at Jaime.

"Jaime?"

There was no reply.

The gun rattled in my hand. I couldn't do it. I couldn't shoot Jaime. We were supposed to be married. How had this happened? How could he just be gone? I turned toward the tree and took one step toward it. I took a deep breath and looked back one last time just as Kellimore reached me, the horde of zombies just a few paces behind.

Jaime sat up.

"Jaime?"

His head snapped as he turned and looked at me. His eyes were moon-white.

"Jaime?"

He opened his mouth. Bloody foam trickled out. I took a step toward him.

"No, you don't," Kellimore told me. He grabbed me around the waist, throwing me over his shoulder, as he reached for the lowest tree branch and pulled us both up. I then felt hands as Tristan pulled me up and across the branches to safety.

LAYLA

"Come on," Cricket said gently, pulling me by the hand.

"No one else made it?" Elle whispered to Kellimore.

"No. Well, I don't think so. I saw this woman in the building. She was opening the gates. I don't know who the hell she was, but she was helping them."

"Where are we going?" Will asked Tristan. "I thought we were headed back to town for the trucks," Will said, casting a glance back toward me.

"I know a safe place. It will take us away from here," Tristan answered.

"Another gate?" Frenchie asked, I heard the suspicion in her voice.

"You were tricked before. I'm here to help you. I will take us from here, take us somewhere safe," Tristan replied.

"That's what they told Layla last time," Tom answered.

"This time it's different," Tristan replied.

I heard their conversation, but I couldn't speak. What had I just seen? What had just happened? Jaime. My Jaime. Gone.

"It'll be all right," Cricket said, wrapping her arm around my waist. "You just hang on. You just hang right on. I...I'm so sorry. I can't imagine. You just hold on to me," she told me.

"Cricket?" Tristan called back.

"I got her," Cricket called in reply.

Tears flooded my eyes. Buddie. Kiki. Summer. Ethel. Now Jaime. My Jaime. My love. Tears slid down my cheeks. All gone. I couldn't save anyone. I'd failed. I'd failed to save the one I loved the most. And worse still, I'd left him behind, to live on like...like that.

"Mommy, look, more fireflies," Susan called.

My eyes blurry with tears, I looked ahead. We had reached the jumble of stones Tristan had showed me when we'd first arrived.

"Wait," I heard Tristan say. There was panic in his voice.

I blinked hard and looked again. Sitting in front of the crevice between the rocks was a fox. In a shimmer of light, the kitsune woman transformed.

"It's her," Kellimore said.

"Sorry, but I can't allow you to pass," the woman told Tristan smartly. The sound of her voice, pleased by her own cleverness, infuriated me.

"You can't stop me. Move aside," he told her. "This is not your place."

"Nor is it theirs," she replied, motioning to us.

"Shoot her," Ariel said, raising her gun, but Tristan motioned for her to be still.

"Nice ward you have there," the kitsune woman said. "Since when did the seelie take in the blood-thirsty?"

"You are a fool. You have no idea what you have done. You've missed it entirely," Tristan told her.

"Killed their kind," she said, motioning to us. "Poisoned the dark fiends. I'd say a job well done," the kitsune woman answered.

There was a rumble in the brush nearby. The smell reached my nose before I heard their terrible groans. A moment later, the undead emerged from the dark forest. Before we even had a chance to process what we were seeing, one of them grabbed Mister Iago and took a massive bite from the little man's head. Blood splattered everywhere.

He went down screaming.

"Oh, I forgot to mention I brought some friends," the woman said with a smile.

Chase and Elle turned and started shooting. Cricket let go of me, and I backed toward Kira and Susan. I'd die on my feet to protect them. If I could just get them into the passageway…this time, they would be safe. Tristan was taking us somewhere protected. We just had to get there.

Kellimore shot toward the undead, but the automatic ran out of ammo. Cursing, he threw it toward the ground and pulled out a handgun.

Darius and Ariel stayed close and pressed back toward the group, shooting the undead who neared us.

"Clear the path or I'll have your head," Tristan told the kitsune woman.

"Uh-uh-uh," she scolded him, her finger wagging. "And start another war between our people and yours? You can't lay a finger on me."

Then, I saw movement and another undead man approached. It was the same undead creature I'd seen at the YMCA, the undead man who had helped me save Jaime and the others, the undead man who'd told me to run. It was looking at the kitsune woman curiously as Tristan and the woman sparred with words.

"Do you hear me?" I called to the man.

The undead man looked at me. *"You!"*

To my surprise, Vella also turned and looked at me.

"She...she led them — us — here. What is she?" the undead man asked me.

"She is the one who killed us all," I told him.

The man's lips curled.

The kitsune woman never even saw him coming. He rushed her with such immense force that he knocked her from her feet and sent her tumbling to the ground before she had a chance to shift. She let out a strange, howling bark as the man ripped into her throat.

"Go," Tristan yelled to us. Pulling Vella and then Cricket, he led them toward the cave. "Go straight through. When you see light, go forward."

Cricket and Vella entered the space, the blue light shimmering all around them, then disappeared.

"Are you certain?" Frenchie asked Tristan, her eyes wet with tears. "My girls..."

Tristan nodded reassuringly then smiled at the girls. "It will be safe."

Tom picked up Kira. "Let's go," he said, then the three of them disappeared into the cave.

Darius, Ariel, and Elle followed behind them.

"Layla, let's go," Tristan said.

Kellimore looked at me, nodded, and then headed into the cave.

The undead closed in.

I closed my eyes.

Tristan took me gently by the arm. "Time to go," he whispered.

I nodded, turned, and followed behind him, entering the cave.

Sweet wind blew from the cave, the scent of flowers, and summer, and sunlight perfumed the breeze. I closed my eyes and soaked it in, expecting the rushing feeling I'd experience the last time, and bracing myself for whatever would come next. In a single instant, before I was swept away, I opened my eyes and looked back at the forest.

There, among the undead who moved in a confused manner, their prey disappearing into the ether, I recognized a familiar silhouette.

"Layla?"

I gasped. "Jaime?"

But the word was lost to the echoing silence.

THANK YOU

I hope you enjoyed *The Shadow Aspect*.
If you would like updates about this series, information
about new releases, and free short stories, please join my
mailing list: http://eepurl.com/OSPDH
Ready for the next adventure? Meet Amelia in *Witch Wood*,
A Harvesting Series Novella, coming October 2015!

ACKNOWLEDGMENTS

With many thanks to Becky Stephens, Naomi Clewett, Liliana Sanches, Nadège Richards, the Airship Stargazer Ground Crew, the Blazing Indie Collective, Carrie Wells, Staci Hart, Michael Hall Jr., and my beloved family.

A FALLING IN DEEP COLLECTION NOVELLA

CHAPTER 1

The first bomb exploded with a flash of white oxygen bubbles. A sharp, piercing sound followed. I felt like my skull would burst. Even though the pain threatened to deafen me, I suppressed my scream. Biting my lip, I tasted blood, and my shimmering blue tail curled. I squinted hard, covering my ears with my hands. My whole body shook, and I knew it wasn't over yet. Five more bombs dropped into the water. The dolphins near the fishing vessel whistled in agony, and then became silent.

I rocked in the water, the ripple of shockwaves rolling past me. Every muscle in my body tensed. When the pain softened, I opened my eyes to see the bottom of the commercial fishing vessel gliding through the water, the prop on slow. Bobbing on the waves, the dolphins floated immobilized. Below the dolphins, tuna huddled, ripe for the picking.

Of course, they weren't all dolphins. Several of the dolphins were, in fact, merdolphins. I scanned the water for my cousin Indigo. King Creon had ordered me to bring her back at once. Something was happening at the grotto. There had been a flurry of preparation, but I didn't know why. It wasn't as if the king shared his plans with me. Why would he? I was an annoyance to him, a constant reminder of his deceased brother who'd ruled before—and better than—him, a brother whose death had bought Creon the throne.

"Ink?" Seaton called. "Are you all right?"

I glanced over at him. The gruff old merman stiffened his back, his dark purple tail uncurling. Small clouds of blood trailed from his ears.

I nodded. "You?"

"They are using seal bombs," he said angrily. "Illegally."

"When did humans ever pay attention to their own laws?" I turned to the others, the small band of scouts who'd come with me. It was times like this that I missed Roald who'd left the ocean for his exile year. He would have had something smart to say to cut the mood. But Roald was not there, and the rest of us were far too serious to make jokes. "Everyone else okay?"

"We'll be fine," Achates, a hulking merman with dark hair and a ruby-red tail, assured me. He squeezed his blades and glared angrily at the boat overhead. There was no one we hated more than the fishermen…well, except the oilmen. It was no wonder the mermaids of old hypnotized and drowned humans for fun. Of course, that was before my great-great-grandfather King Tricus outlawed siren song. His daughter, Princess Tigonea, had tried to use siren song against her father in an attempt to usurp power. We mermaids still suffered for her failed regicide.

I scanned the water. The bubbles caused by the blasts faded into halos at the surface. Some of the dolphins and the merdolphins, started to recover. We needed to get to them.

The tuna clustered under the dolphins. Atlantic tuna were easy to find if you knew where to look. If you hunted dolphins, you found tuna. The fishermen began dropping their purse-shaped net. It drifted downward like a dark haze.

"Let's go," I called, gripping my blades.

We swam quickly toward the pod, careful to stay far enough below the surface to remain unseen. By sonar, we'd just look like another pod of dolphins. Humans knew nothing about the deep. As long as we were cautious, they'd never see us.

As we drew closer, I noticed that some of the older dolphins had been killed. They floated like plastic bottles on the surface, their white bellies facing the sun. Others kicked and tried to recover from the deafening blast, swimming away in confusion. The dolphins' blood clouded the water, filling my nostrils. This was nothing short of murder.

"Indigo," I called, careful not to sound too loudly. Hearing me, several of the merdolphins turned and swam our direction. I could see from their awkward movements that many of them were injured. Indigo, whom I finally spotted among the dolphin pod, had shapeshifted into dolphin form. Preoccupied with one of the mother dolphins, she had not heard me.

"Can you get them home?" I asked Achates, referring to the injured mers, several of whom had started to shift back to their natural mermaid or merman form.

"Yes, My Lady," he said as he and two of the other scouts led the wounded mers away.

Overhead, the boat motored in a wide circle: halfway done. Soon they would close the net, and we'd be trapped inside. We needed to work fast.

I motioned to Seaton, and then we shot through the water. "Indigo," I called.

She turned and whistled to me in panic. Once we got close, I could see the problem. The mother dolphin had started to calf and wouldn't be moved.

"Ill-omened," Seaton grumbled. "Nothing can be done here, Lady Indigo. You have to go. They are dropping the net."

Indigo shook her head, and then stared at me, making direct eye contact. Against my better judgment, I knew what had to be done.

"We have to cut the net," I told Seaton.

"Dangerous work," the merman said and grinned. "Best get to it."

"In the meantime, try to convince her," I told Indigo, and then Seaton and I set off. I grabbed the net, feeling the rough, human-made object in my hands. It didn't matter how many times drywalkers—mers who could shift into human form, mers like me—told me that humans were kind. All I saw was the death and filth and destruction they wrought. They were little more than barbarian apes. Land brought death. Just ask my mother. Who knew where her corpse lay rotting in the dirt? But that death had not been caused by humans. The Gulf tribe had killed my mother. She'd been a casualty of our war. I barely remembered her anymore, just the shadowy memories of her red hair, her dainty drywalker tribal mark, and the way she sang with a low cadence. How unlike her I was with my massive swirling drywalker tribal covering my back. While our marks were different, we were the same lot in life. Now it was my turn to walk on terra firma. My exile year had arrived. That night I would begin my drywalk. I shuddered at the thought, and then turned back to my task. It didn't do me any good to think about it now. Moonrise would be here soon enough.

I stabbed my blade into the net and jerked it. The net resisted. I yanked hard and soon the metal began to cut. Below me, the massive tuna huddled together. I could taste their fear in the water. Poor beasts. We fed on them too but not in such a barbarous way. With a little luck, I'd have them out of there as well.

As I jerked my knife, I stared at the boat motoring overhead. Seaton was right. Everything about this fishing practice was illegal. The purse-seine fishing method they were using had been outlawed years ago. Disgusting. At least merpeople honored their laws, even when we didn't like it.

The torn net wagged with the motion of the waves. As I worked, anger welling up in me. If it hadn't meant having their refuse in my waters, I could just sink their boat and drown them all. It was, after all, instinctual for me to want their death. While our law forbad using siren song, which was nothing more than tuning of sound resonance, I still felt the ancestral tug in me. I would have loved to purr a sweet song and pull them down into a murky death. I could almost hear the tune in the back of my head, humming from an ancient source. The song of the siren was nearly lost now, its banishment causing it to fade from common use or knowledge. I closed my eyes. With just a few notes, it would all be done.

"Ink?" Seaton called.

I opened my eyes. *Careful, Ink.* "Good. Almost there." I glanced back at Indigo. She'd moved the mother dolphin deeper into the water, away from the surface, and had shifted back into mermaid form. Her blueish hair, befitting her name, made a halo around her. She was using merdolphin magic to dazzle the creature, talking in low melodious tones that echoed softly through the water.

Seaton stopped just above me.

"Got it," I said, then slid my blade upward. The net broke in half, wagging like seaweed in the waves.

Seaton and I swam to Indigo who was guiding the mother dolphin, holding her gently by the flipper. From above, there was a terrible groan, then a screech as the gears on the winch sprang to life. The net wall moved like it was alive, the tentacles of a great sea monster closing in on us.

"We must hurry," Seaton said.

Moving quickly, we swam through the tear and out of the net, back into the safety of the open ocean.

The gears on the winch lurched. Water pressure pulled the tear, causing the net to rip wide open. The tuna rushed free. I tread for a moment, stopping to watch the sight as Indigo guided the mother dolphin into the dark water below us.

"The pup is coming," Indigo called from the blackness below.

Above, the bottom of the boat rocked, unsteadied by the broken net. The winch slowly reeled the mesh out of the water. It looked like a dead thing, a man-made monster fished out of the living ocean. As the fishermen moved along the rail of the ship, their images were weirdly distorted against the surface of the water. With all my willpower, I sucked in the death-dealing note that wanted to escape from my lips. The massive swirling tribal mark on my back started to feel prickly and warm. Harnessing myself in, I reminded myself that it was forbidden. I turned and swam into the shadowy deep.

Catch *Ink: A Mermaid Romance* on Amazon.com

62941579R00175

Made in the USA
Lexington, KY
22 April 2017